THE MERCHANT OF VENICE

DOVER THRIFT EDITIONS

William Shakespeare

DOVER PUBLICATIONS
GARDEN CITY, NEW YORK

DOVER THRIFT EDITIONS

GENERAL EDITOR: STANLEY APPELBAUM
EDITOR OF THIS VOLUME: CANDACE WARD

Performance

This Dover Thrift Edition may be used in its entirety, in adaptation or in any other way for theatrical productions, professional and amateur, in the United States, without fee, permission or acknowledgment. (This may not apply outside of the United States, as copyright conditions may vary.)

Bibliographical Note

This Dover edition, first published in 1995, contains the unabridged text of *The Merchant of Venice* as published in Volume II of *The Caxton Edition of the Complete Works of William Shakespeare*, Caxton Publishing Company, London, n.d. The Note and explanatory footnotes were prepared specially for this edition.

Library of Congress Cataloging-in-Publication Data

Shakespeare, William, 1564–1616.
    The merchant of Venice / William Shakespeare.
        p.   cm. — (Dover thrift editions)
    Text taken from The Caxton edition of the complete works of William Shakespeare, v. 2.
      ISBN-13: 978-0-486-28492-7
      ISBN-10: 0-486-28492-1

    1. Jews—Italy—Venice—Drama.   I. Title.   II. Series.
PR2825.A1   1995
822.3'3—dc20
                                                            95-10121
                                                            CIP

Manufactured in the United States of America
28492119   2023
www.doverpublications.com

NOTE

The Merchant of Venice was probably written about 1596. Though a comedy, the play includes tragic elements and is wrought with dramatic tension. The primary plot revolves around two pairs of lovers, Portia and Bassanio, and Jessica and Lorenzo. But it is the relationship between Antonio, the merchant of Venice, and the moneylender Shylock that unites the play and provides the central conflict. Briefly, Antonio has borrowed money from Shylock in order to help Bassanio court Portia; the terms of the bond are such that if he cannot repay the loan within three months, he must give Shylock a pound of his flesh.

The unsympathetic portrayal of the Jewish moneylender is a troubling element in Shakespeare's play and it is often read as a reflection of attitudes in England at the end of the sixteenth century. One contemporary incident that might have influenced Shakespeare's characterization of Shylock involved Queen Elizabeth's personal physician, the Portuguese Jew Roderigo López. López was appointed interpreter and guardian of Antonio Pérez, an exile from Philip II's Spanish court. After becoming involved in a series of court intrigues, including an unsuccessful plot to assassinate Pérez, López was implicated in an attempt to poison the Queen. Although the Queen herself was unconvinced of his guilt, under pressure from the earl of Essex she signed López's death warrant. He was publicly executed (hanged, drawn and quartered) on June 7, 1594. The jeering crowd that witnessed the execution, the popularity of Shakespeare's play and the successful revival of Marlowe's *The Jew of Malta* reveal the extent of anti-Jewish sentiment at the time.

If Elizabethan audiences were unsympathetic toward Shylock, succeeding ones were drawn to him. Writing in the early nineteenth century, William Hazlitt saw "a strong, quick, and deep sense of justice

iii

mixed up with the gall and bitterness of [Shylock's] resentment. . . . [W]e
pity him, and think him hardly dealt with by his judges." Bernhard Ten
Brink allowed that Shylock's punishment for the most part is "nothing
more than poetic justice." But, he adds, upon Antonio's stipulation that
Shylock convert to Christianity, "our feelings justly rebel. . . . Shylock
has come too close to us, we have learned to know too intimately the
grounds of his hatred, of the intensity of his resentment, his figure has
become too humanly significant and the misfortune which overtakes
him appeals too deeply to our sympathies, to permit us to be reconciled
to the idea that his fate, which moves us so tragically, should be con-
ceived as otherwise than as a tragedy."

CONTENTS

DRAMATIS PERSONÆ

THE DUKE OF VENICE.
THE PRINCE OF MOROCCO,⎱ suitors to Portia.
THE PRINCE OF ARRAGON, ⎰
ANTONIO, a merchant of Venice.
BASSANIO, his friend, suitor likewise to Portia.
SALANIO,
SALARINO, ⎱
GRATIANO, ⎰ friends to Antonio and Bassanio.
SALERIO,
LORENZO, in love with Jessica.
SHYLOCK, a rich Jew.
TUBAL, a Jew, his friend.
LAUNCELOT GOBBO, the clown, servant to Shylock.
OLD GOBBO, father to Launcelot.
LEONARDO, servant to Bassanio.
BALTHASAR, ⎱ servants to Portia.
STEPHANO, ⎰
PORTIA, a rich heiress.
NERISSA, her waiting-maid.
JESSICA, daughter to Shylock.

Magnificoes of Venice, Officers of the Court of Justice, Gaoler,
Servants to Portia, and other Attendants.

SCENE — *Partly at Venice, and partly at Belmont, the seat of Portia,*
on the Continent

ACT I.

SCENE I. *Venice. A Street.*

Enter ANTONIO, SALARINO, *and* SALANIO

ANT.　In sooth, I know not why I am so sad:
　　It wearies me; you say it wearies you;
　　But how I caught it, found it, or came by it,
　　What stuff 't is made of, whereof it is born,
　　I am to learn;
　　And such a want-wit sadness makes of me,
　　That I have much ado to know myself.
SALAR.　Your mind is tossing on the ocean;
　　There, where your argosies with portly sail,
　　Like signiors and rich burghers on the flood,
　　Or, as it were, the pageants[1] of the sea,
　　Do overpeer the petty traffickers,
　　That curt'sy to them, do them reverence,
　　As they fly by them with their woven wings.
SALAN.　Believe me, sir, had I such venture forth,
　　The better part of my affections would
　　Be with my hopes abroad. I should be still
　　Plucking the grass, to know where sits the wind;
　　Peering in maps for ports, and piers, and roads;
　　And every object, that might make me fear

---

1. *pageants*] An allusion to the huge, towering machines in the shape of castles, dragons, giants, and the like, which formed part of ancient shows, and were drawn on ceremonial occasions through the streets.

1

    Misfortune to my ventures, out of doubt
    Would make me sad.

SALAR.   My wind, cooling my broth,
    Would blow me to an ague, when I thought
    What harm a wind too great at sea might do.
    I should not see the sandy hour-glass run,
    But I should think of shallows and of flats,
    And see my wealthy Andrew[2] dock'd in sand
    Vailing her high top lower than her ribs
    To kiss her burial.[3] Should I go to church
    And see the holy edifice of stone,
    And not bethink me straight of dangerous rocks,
    Which touching but my gentle vessel's side
    Would scatter all her spices on the stream,
    Enrobe the roaring waters with my silks;
    And, in a word, but even now worth this,
    And now worth nothing? Shall I have the thought
    To think on this; and shall I lack the thought,
    That such a thing bechanced would make me sad?
    But tell not me; I know, Antonio
    Is sad to think upon his merchandise.

ANT.   Believe me, no: I thank my fortune for it,
    My ventures are not in one bottom trusted,
    Nor to one place; nor is my whole estate
    Upon the fortune of this present year:
    Therefore my merchandise makes me not sad.

SALAR.   Why, then you are in love.

ANT.   Fie, fie!

SALAR.   Not in love neither? Then let us say you are sad,
    Because you are not merry: and 't were as easy
    For you to laugh, and leap, and say you are merry,
    Because you are not sad. Now, by two-headed Janus,[4]
    Nature hath framed strange fellows in her time:
    Some that will evermore peep through their eyes,

---

2. *Andrew*] the name of a ship.
3. *kiss her burial*] touch her burial place, sink.
4. *two-headed Janus*] The Roman god Janus was often depicted with two faces.

And laugh like parrots at a bag-piper;
And other of such vinegar aspect,
That they 'll not show their teeth in way of smile,
Though Nestor[5] swear the jest be laughable.

Enter BASSANIO, LORENZO, *and* GRATIANO

SALAN.   Here comes Bassanio, your most noble kinsman,
Gratiano, and Lorenzo. Fare ye well:
We leave you now with better company.
SALAR.   I would have stay'd till I had made you merry,
If worthier friends had not prevented me.
ANT.   Your worth is very dear in my regard.
I take it, your own business calls on you,
And you embrace the occasion to depart.
SALAR.   Good morrow, my good lords.
BASS.   Good signiors both, when shall we laugh? say, when?
You grow exceeding strange: must it be so?
SALAR.   We 'll make our leisures to attend on yours.
                                    [*Exeunt* SALARINO *and* SALANIO.]
LOR.   My Lord Bassanio, since you have found Antonio,
We two will leave you: but, at dinner-time,
I pray you, have in mind where we must meet.
BASS.   I will not fail you.
GRA.   You look not well, Signior Antonio;
You have too much respect upon the world:[6]
They lose it that do buy it with much care:
Believe me, you are marvellously changed.
ANT.   I hold the world but as the world, Gratiano;
A stage, where every man must play a part,
And mine a sad one.
GRA.   Let me play the fool:
With mirth and laughter let old wrinkles come;
And let my liver rather heat with wine
Than my heart cool with mortifying groans.

---

5. *Nestor*] a king of Pylos who served in his old age as a counselor to the Greeks at Troy.
6. *respect upon the world*] worldly care, anxiety.

Why should a man, whose blood is warm within,
Sit like his grandsire cut in alabaster?
Sleep when he wakes, and creep into the jaundice
By being peevish? I tell thee what, Antonio —
I love thee, and it is my love that speaks, —
There are a sort of men, whose visages
Do cream and mantle like a standing pond;[7]
And do a wilful stillness entertain,
With purpose to be dress'd in an opinion
Of wisdom, gravity, profound conceit;
As who should say, "I am Sir Oracle,
And, when I ope my lips, let no dog bark!"
O my Antonio, I do know of these,
That therefore only are reputed wise
For saying nothing; when, I am very sure,
If they should speak, would almost damn those ears,
Which, hearing them, would call their brothers fools.
I 'll tell thee more of this another time:
But fish not, with this melancholy bait,
For this fool gudgeon,[8] this opinion.
Come, good Lorenzo. Fare ye well awhile:
I 'll end my exhortation after dinner.

LOR.   Well, we will leave you, then, till dinner-time:
I must be one of these same dumb wise men,
For Gratiano never lets me speak.

GRA.   Well, keep me company but two years moe,
Thou shalt not know the sound of thine own tongue.

ANT.   Farewell: I 'll grow a talker for this gear.[9]

GRA.   Thanks, i' faith; for silence is only commendable
In a neat's tongue[10] dried, and a maid not vendible.

[*Exeunt* GRATIANO *and* LORENZO.]

ANT.   Is that any thing now?

---

7. *Do cream ... pond*] Acquire the cream-like mantle or coating that gathers on a stagnant pool.
8. *gudgeon*] a small fish that is easily caught; here, a person easily duped.
9. *gear*] stuff, business.
10. *neat's tongue*] "neat" refers to horned cattle; beef tongue.

BASS.   Gratiano speaks an infinite deal of nothing, more than any man
    in all Venice. His reasons are as two grains of wheat hid in two
    bushels of chaff: you shall seek all day ere you find them: and when
    you have them, they are not worth the search.
ANT.   Well, tell me now, what lady is the same
    To whom you swore a secret pilgrimage,
    That you to-day promised to tell me of?
BASS.   'T is not unknown to you, Antonio,
    How much I have disabled mine estate,
    By something showing a more swelling port
    Than my faint means would grant continuance:
    Nor do I now make moan to be abridged
    From such a noble rate; but my chief care
    Is, to come fairly off from the great debts,
    Wherein my time, something too prodigal,
    Hath left me gaged. To you, Antonio,
    I owe the most, in money and in love;
    And from your love I have a warranty
    To unburthen all my plots and purposes
    How to get clear of all the debts I owe.
ANT.   I pray you, good Bassanio, let me know it;
    And if it stand, as you yourself still do,
    Within the eye of honour, be assured,
    My purse, my person, my extremest means,
    Lie all unlock'd to your occasions.
BASS.   In my school-days, when I had lost one shaft,
    I shot his fellow of the self-same flight
    The self-same way with more advised watch,
    To find the other forth; and by adventuring both,
    I oft found both: I urge this childhood proof,
    Because what follows is pure innocence.
    I owe you much; and, like a wilful youth,
    That which I owe is lost: but if you please
    To shoot another arrow that self way
    Which you did shoot the first, I do not doubt,
    As I will watch the aim, or to find both,
    Or bring your latter hazard back again,

      And thankfully rest debtor for the first.

ANT.   You know me well; and herein spend but time
      To wind about my love with circumstance;
      And out of doubt you do me now more wrong
      In making question of my uttermost,
      Than if you had made waste of all I have:
      Then do but say to me what I should do,
      That in your knowledge may by me be done,
      And I am prest[11] unto it: therefore, speak.

BASS.   In Belmont is a lady richly left;
      And she is fair, and, fairer than that word,
      Of wondrous virtues: sometimes from her eyes
      I did receive fair speechless messages:
      Her name is Portia; nothing undervalued
      To Cato's daughter, Brutus' Portia:
      Nor is the wide world ignorant of her worth;
      For the four winds blow in from every coast
      Renowned suitors: and her sunny locks
      Hang on her temples like a golden fleece;
      Which makes her seat of Belmont Colchos' strond,[12]
      And many Jasons come in quest of her.
      O my Antonio, had I but the means
      To hold a rival place with one of them,
      I have a mind presages me such thrift,[13]
      That I should questionless be fortunate!

ANT.   Thou know'st that all my fortunes are at sea;
      Neither have I money, nor commodity
      To raise a present sum: therefore go forth;
      Try what my credit can in Venice do:
      That shall be rack'd, even to the uttermost,
      To furnish thee to Belmont, to fair Portia.
      Go, presently inquire, and so will I,

---

11. *prest*] ready, from the French, *prêt*.
12. *Colchos' strond*] Colchis was the country of the golden fleece; strond is "strand," or beach, shore.
13. *such thrift*] such thriving, good success.

Where money is; and I no question make,
To have it of my trust, or for my sake.   [*Exeunt.*]

SCENE II. *Belmont. A room in* PORTIA'S *house.*

Enter PORTIA *and* NERISSA

POR. By my troth, Nerissa, my little body is aweary of this great world.

NER. You would be, sweet madam, if your miseries were in the same
abundance as your good fortunes are: and yet, for aught I see, they
are as sick that surfeit with too much, as they that starve with
nothing. It is no mean happiness, therefore, to be seated in the
mean: superfluity comes sooner by white hairs; but competency
lives longer.

POR. Good sentences,[1] and well pronounced.

NER. They would be better, if well followed.

POR. If to do were as easy as to know what were good to do, chapels
had been churches, and poor men's cottages princes' palaces. It is a
good divine that follows his own instructions: I can easier teach
twenty what were good to be done, than be one of the twenty to
follow mine own teaching. The brain may devise laws for the
blood; but a hot temper leaps o'er a cold decree: such a hare is
madness the youth, to skip o'er the meshes of good counsel the
cripple. But this reasoning is not in the fashion to choose me a
husband. O me, the word "choose"! I may neither choose whom I
would, nor refuse whom I dislike; so is the will of a living daughter
curbed by the will of a dead father. Is it not hard, Nerissa, that I
cannot choose one, nor refuse none?

NER. Your father was ever virtuous; and holy men, at their death, have
good inspirations: therefore, the lottery, that he hath devised in

---

1. *sentences*] maxims.

these three chests of gold, silver, and lead, — whereof who chooses his meaning chooses you, — will, no doubt, never be chosen by any rightly, but one who shall rightly love. But what warmth is there in your affection towards any of these princely suitors that are already come?

POR. I pray thee, over-name them; and as thou namest them, I will describe them; and, according to my description, level at[2] my affection.

NER. First, there is the Neapolitan prince.

POR. Ay, that's a colt indeed, for he doth nothing but talk of his horse; and he makes it a great appropriation to his own good parts, that he can shoe him himself. I am much afeard my lady his mother played false with a smith.

NER. Then there is the County Palatine.

POR. He doth nothing but frown; as who should say, "if you will not have me, choose:" he hears merry tales, and smiles not: I fear he will prove the weeping philosopher[3] when he grows old, being so full of unmannerly sadness in his youth. I had rather be married to a death's-head with a bone in his mouth than to either of these. God defend me from these two!

NER. How say you by the French lord, Monsieur Le Bon?

POR. God made him, and therefore let him pass for a man. In truth, I know it is a sin to be a mocker: but, he! — why, he hath a horse better than the Neapolitan's; a better bad habit of frowning than the Count Palatine: he is every man in no man; if a throstle sing, he falls straight a capering: he will fence with his own shadow: if I should marry him, I should marry twenty husbands. If he would despise me, I would forgive him; for if he love me to madness, I shall never requite him.

NER. What say you, then, to Falconbridge, the young baron of England?

POR. You know I say nothing to him; for he understands not me, nor I him: he hath neither Latin, French, nor Italian; and you will come

---

2. *level at*] aim at, guess at.
3. *weeping philosopher*] An allusion to the Greek philosopher, Heraclitus, who is usually contrasted with Democritus, "the laughing philosopher."

into the court and swear that I have a poor pennyworth in the English. He is a proper man's picture; but, alas, who can converse with a dumb-show? How oddly he is suited! I think he bought his doublet in Italy, his round hose in France, his bonnet in Germany, and his behaviour every where.

NER.   What think you of the Scottish lord, his neighbour?

POR.   That he hath a neighbourly charity in him; for he borrowed a box of the ear of the Englishman, and swore he would pay him again when he was able: I think the Frenchman became his surety, and sealed under[4] for another.

NER.   How like you the young German, the Duke of Saxony's nephew?

POR.   Very vilely in the morning, when he is sober; and most vilely in the afternoon, when he is drunk: when he is best, he is a little worse than a man; and when he is worst, he is little better than a beast: an the worst fall that ever fell, I hope I shall make shift to go without him.

NER.   If he should offer to choose, and choose the right casket, you should refuse to perform your father's will, if you should refuse to accept him.

POR.   Therefore, for fear of the worst, I pray thee, set a deep glass of Rhenish wine on the contrary casket; for, if the devil be within and that temptation without, I know he will choose it. I will do any thing, Nerissa, ere I'll be married to a sponge.

NER.   You need not fear, lady, the having any of these lords: they have acquainted me with their determinations; which is, indeed, to return to their home, and to trouble you with no more suit, unless you may be won by some other sort than your father's imposition, depending on the caskets.

POR.   If I live to be as old as Sibylla,[5] I will die as chaste as Diana, unless I be obtained by the manner of my father's will. I am glad this parcel of wooers are so reasonable; for there is not one among

---

4. *sealed under*] A legal expression implying that the bond or surety was entered into vicariously, in behalf of some other person who was responsible.

5. *Sibylla*] An obvious reference to the story of Sibylla, the Cumæan Sibyl, in Ovid's *Metamorphoses*, XIV, where Apollo promises her as many years of life as the grains of sand she holds in her hand.

them but I dote on his very absence; and I pray God grant them a fair departure.

NER.   Do you not remember, lady, in your father's time, a Venetian, a scholar, and a soldier, that came hither in company of the Marquis of Montferrat?

POR.   Yes, yes, it was Bassanio; as I think he was so called.

NER.   True, madam: he, of all the men that ever my foolish eyes looked upon, was the best deserving a fair lady.

POR.   I remember him well; and I remember him worthy of thy praise.

Enter a Serving-man

How now! what news?

SERV.   The four strangers[6] seek for you, madam, to take their leave: and there is a forerunner come from a fifth, the Prince of Morocco; who brings word, the prince his master will be here to-night.

POR.   If I could bid the fifth welcome with so good a heart as I can bid the other four farewell, I should be glad of his approach: if he have the condition of a saint and the complexion of a devil, I had rather he should shrive me than wive me.
Come, Nerissa. Sirrah, go before.
Whiles we shut the gates upon one wooer, another knocks at the door.   [*Exeunt.*]

SCENE III. *Venice. A public place.*

Enter BASSANIO *and* SHYLOCK

SHY.   Three thousand ducats;[1] well.

---

6. *The four strangers*] Portia has already described the suitors who are about to take leave of her as six in number. "*Four*," which is repeated a few lines later, is either a misprint for *six*, or this passage may present an unrevised relic of a first draft of the play.

1. *Three thousand ducats*] "Ducat" was the name of a Venetian coin cast both in gold and silver. The gold ducat was worth about ten shillings, and the silver ducat under five

BASS.   Ay, sir, for three months.

SHY.   For three months; well.

BASS.   For the which, as I told you, Antonio shall be bound.

SHY.   Antonio shall become bound; well.

BASS.   May you stead me? will you pleasure me? shall I know your
        answer?

SHY.   Three thousand ducats for three months, and Antonio bound.

BASS.   Your answer to that.

SHY.   Antonio is a good man.

BASS.   Have you heard any imputation to the contrary?

SHY.   Ho, no, no, no, no: my meaning, in saying he is a good man, is to
        have you understand me, that he is sufficient. Yet his means are in
        supposition: he hath an argosy bound to Tripolis, another to the
        Indies; I understand, moreover, upon the Rialto,[2] he hath a third at
        Mexico, a fourth for England, and other ventures he hath, squan-
        dered abroad. But ships are but boards, sailors but men: there be
        land-rats and water-rats, water-thieves and land-thieves, I mean
        pirates; and then there is the peril of waters, winds, and rocks. The
        man is, notwithstanding, sufficient. Three thousand ducats; I think
        I may take his bond.

BASS.   Be assured you may.

SHY.   I will be assured I may; and, that I may be assured, I will bethink
        me. May I speak with Antonio?

BASS.   If it please you to dine with us.

SHY.   Yes, to smell pork; to eat of the habitation which your prophet the
        Nazarite conjured the devil into. I will buy with you, sell with you,
        talk with you, walk with you, and so following; but I will not eat
        with you, drink with you, nor pray with you. What news on the
        Rialto? Who is he comes here?

Enter ANTONIO

BASS.   This is Signior Antonio.

---

shillings. Like other Elizabethan writers, Shakespeare seems to use the term here to mean a
coin of great worth without attaching to it a very precise value.

2. *Rialto*] The Venetian financial district, similar to the London Exchange. The famous
bridge at Venice, called after the Exchange, Ponte di Rialto, was not built until 1591.

SHY.   [*Aside*] How like a fawning publican he looks!
    I hate him for he is a Christian;
    But more for that in low simplicity
    He lends out money gratis and brings down
    The rate of usance[3] here with us in Venice.
    If I can catch him once upon the hip,
    I will feed fat the ancient grudge I bear him.
    He hates our sacred nation; and he rails,
    Even there where merchants most do congregate,
    On me, my bargains, and my well-won thrift,
    Which he calls interest. Cursed be my tribe,
    If I forgive him!
BASS.   Shylock, do you hear?
SHY.   I am debating of my present store;
    And, by the near guess of my memory,
    I cannot instantly raise up the gross
    Of full three thousand ducats. What of that?
    Tubal, a wealthy Hebrew of my tribe,
    Will furnish me. But soft! how many months
    Do you desire? [*To Ant.*] Rest you fair, good signior;
    Your worship was the last man in our mouths.
ANT.   Shylock, although I neither lend nor borrow,
    By taking nor by giving of excess,[4]
    Yet, to supply the ripe wants of my friend,
    I 'll break a custom. Is he yet possess'd
    How much ye would?
SHY.   Ay, ay, three thousand ducats.
ANT.   And for three months.
SHY.   I had forgot; three months, you told me so.
    Well then, your bond; and let me see; but hear you;
    Methought you said you neither lend nor borrow
    Upon advantage.
ANT.   I do never use it.

---

3. *usance*] interest paid on money lent.
4. *excess*] interest.

SHY.   When Jacob grazed his uncle Laban's sheep, — [5]
     This Jacob from our holy Abram was,
     As his wise mother wrought in his behalf,
     The third possessor; ay, he was the third, —
ANT.   And what of him? did he take interest?
SHY.   No, not take interest; not, as you would say,
     Directly interest: mark what Jacob did.
     When Laban and himself were compromised
     That all the eanlings[6] which were streak'd and pied
     Should fall as Jacob's hire, the ewes, being rank,
     In the end of Autumn turned to the rams;
     And when the work of generation was
     Between these woolly breeders in the act,
     The skilful shepherd peel'd me certain wands,
     And, in the doing of the deed of kind,
     He stuck them up before the fulsome ewes,
     Who, then conceiving, did in eanling time
     Fall parti-colour'd lambs, and those were Jacob's.
     This was a way to thrive, and he was blest:
     And thrift is blessing, if men steal it not.
ANT.   This was a venture, sir, that Jacob served for;
     A thing not in his power to bring to pass,
     But sway'd and fashion'd by the hand of heaven.
     Was this inserted to make interest good?
     Or is your gold and silver ewes and rams?
SHY.   I cannot tell; I make it breed as fast:
     But note me, signior.
ANT.   Mark you this, Bassanio,
     The devil can cite Scripture for his purpose.
     An evil soul, producing holy witness,
     Is like a villain with a smiling cheek;
     A goodly apple rotten at the heart:
     O, what a goodly outside falsehood hath!

---

   5. *When Jacob grazed . . . steal it not.*] Shakespeare here paraphrases and interprets the
     passage from *Genesis* 30:37 and following.
   6. *eanlings*] newborn lambs.

SHY. Three thousand ducats; 't is a good round sum.
  Three months from twelve; then, let me see; the rate —
ANT. Well, Shylock, shall we be beholding to you?
SHY. Signior Antonio, many a time and oft
  In the Rialto you have rated me
  About my moneys and my usances:
  Still have I borne it with a patient shrug;
  For sufferance is the badge of all our tribe.
  You call me misbeliever, cut-throat dog,
  And spit upon my Jewish gaberdine,
  And all for use of that which is mine own.
  Well then, it now appears you need my help:
  Go to, then; you come to me, and you say
  "Shylock, we would have moneys:" you say so;
  You, that did void your rheum upon my beard,
  And foot me as you spurn a stranger cur
  Over your threshold: moneys is your suit.
  What should I say to you? Should I not say
  "Hath a dog money? is it possible
  A cur can lend three thousand ducats?" or
  Shall I bend low and in a bondman's key,
  With bated breath and whispering humbleness,
  Say this, —
  "Fair sir, you spit on me on Wednesday last;
  You spurn'd me such a day; another time
  You call'd me dog; and for these courtesies
  I 'll lend you thus much moneys"?
ANT. I am as like to call thee so again,
  To spit on thee again, to spurn thee too.
  If thou wilt lend this money, lend it not
  As to thy friends; for when did friendship take
  A breed[7] for barren metal of his friend?
  But lend it rather to thine enemy;
  Who if he break, thou mayst with better face
  Exact the penalty.

---

7. *breed*] offspring; used figuratively here for interest.

SHY.   Why, look you, how you storm!
    I would be friends with you, and have your love,
    Forget the shames that you have stain'd me with,
    Supply your present wants, and take no doit[8]
    Of usance for my moneys, and you 'll not hear me:
    This is kind I offer.
BASS.   This were kindness.
SHY.   This kindness will I show.
    Go with me to a notary, seal me there
    Your single bond;[9] and, in a merry sport,
    If you repay me not on such a day,
    In such a place, such sum or sums as are
    Express'd in the condition, let the forfeit
    Be nominated for an equal pound
    Of your fair flesh, to be cut off and taken
    In what part of your body pleaseth me.
ANT.   Content, i' faith: I 'll seal to such a bond,
    And say there is much kindness in the Jew.
BASS.   You shall not seal to such a bond for me:
    I 'll rather dwell in my necessity.
ANT.   Why, fear not, man; I will not forfeit it:
    Within these two months, that 's a month before
    This bond expires, I do expect return
    Of thrice three times the value of this bond.
SHY.   O father Abram, what these Christians are,
    Whose own hard dealings teaches them suspect
    The thoughts of others! Pray you, tell me this;
    If he should break his day, what should I gain
    By the exaction of the forfeiture?
    A pound of man's flesh taken from a man
    Is not so estimable, profitable neither,
    As flesh of muttons, beefs, or goats. I say,
    To buy his favour, I extend this friendship:

---

8. *doit*] the smallest piece of money, a trifle.
9. *single bond*] a bond involving one person exclusively; an engagement, responsibility for
   which cannot be devolved on another.

If he will take it, so; if not, adieu;
And, for my love, I pray you wrong me not.

ANT.   Yes, Shylock, I will seal unto this bond.

SHY.   Then meet me forthwith at the notary's;
Give him direction for this merry bond;
And I will go and purse the ducats straight;
See to my house, left in the fearful guard
Of an unthrifty knave; and presently
I will be with you.

ANT.   Hie thee, gentle Jew.   [*Exit* SHYLOCK.]
The Hebrew will turn Christian: he grows kind.

BASS.   I like not fair terms and a villain's mind.

ANT.   Come on: in this there can be no dismay;
My ships come home a month before the day.   [*Exeunt.*]

ACT II.

SCENE I. *Belmont. A room in* PORTIA'S *house.*

Flourish of Cornets. Enter the PRINCE OF MOROCCO *and his train;* PORTIA, NERISSA, *and others attending*

MOR.   Mislike me not for my complexion,
     The shadow'd livery of the burnish'd sun,
     To whom I am a neighbour and near bred.
     Bring me the fairest creature northward born,
     Where Phœbus' fire scarce thaws the icicles,
     And let us make incision for your love,
     To prove whose blood is reddest, his or mine.
     I tell thee, lady, this aspect of mine
     Hath fear'd the valiant: by my love, I swear
     The best-regarded virgins of our clime
     Have loved it too: I would not change this hue,
     Except to steal your thoughts, my gentle queen.
POR.   In terms of choice I am not solely led
     By nice direction of a maiden's eyes;
     Besides, the lottery of my destiny
     Bars me the right of voluntary choosing:
     But if my father had not scanted me
     And hedged me by his wit, to yield myself
     His wife who wins me by that means I told you,
     Yourself, renowned prince, then stood as fair
     As any comer I have look'd on yet
     For my affection.

MOR.   Even for that I thank you:
    Therefore, I pray you, lead me to the caskets,
    To try my fortune. By this scimitar
    That slew the Sophy and a Persian prince
    That won three fields of Sultan Solyman,[1]
    I would outstare the sternest eyes that look,
    Outbrave the heart most daring on the earth,
    Pluck the young sucking cubs from the she-bear,
    Yea, mock the lion when he roars for prey,
    To win thee, lady. But, alas the while!
    If Hercules and Lichas[2] play at dice
    Which is the better man, the greater throw
    May turn by fortune from the weaker hand
    So is Alcides[3] beaten by his page;
    And so may I, blind fortune leading me,
    Miss that which one unworthier may attain,
    And die with grieving.
POR.   You must take your chance;
    And either not attempt to choose at all,
    Or swear before you choose, if you choose wrong,
    Never speak to lady afterward
    In way of marriage: therefore be advised.
MOR.   Nor will not. Come, bring me unto my chance.
POR.   First, forward to the temple: after dinner
    Your hazard shall be made.
MOR.   Good fortune then!
    To make me blest or cursed'st among men.

                                [Cornets, and exeunt.]

---

1. *Sophy . . . Solyman*] The "Sophy" was a title commonly bestowed on the Shah or Emperor of Persia. Suleiman the Magnificent, the greatest of the sultans of the Ottoman Empire, was defeated in an attack on Persia in 1535.
2. *Lichas*] The servant of Hercules who unwittingly brought him the poisoned shirt of Nessus, which caused the hero's death.
3. *Alcides*] Hercules.

SCENE II. *Venice. A street.*

Enter LAUNCELOT

LAUN.   Certainly my conscience will serve me to run from this Jew my master. The fiend is at mine elbow, and tempts me, saying to me, "Gobbo, Launcelot Gobbo, good Launcelot," or "good Gobbo," or "good Launcelot Gobbo, use your legs, take the start, run away." My conscience says, "No; take heed, honest Launcelot; take heed, honest Gobbo," or, as aforesaid, "honest Launcelot Gobbo, do not run; scorn running with thy heels." Well, the most courageous fiend bids me pack: "Via!" says the fiend; "away!" says the fiend; "for the heavens, rouse up a brave mind," says the fiend, "and run." Well, my conscience, hanging about the neck of my heart, says very wisely to me, "My honest friend Launcelot, being an honest man's son," — or rather an honest woman's son; — for, indeed, my father did something smack, something grow to, he had a kind of taste; — well, my conscience says, "Launcelot, budge not." "Budge," says the fiend. "Budge not," says my conscience. "Conscience," say I, "you counsel well;" "Fiend," say I, "you counsel well:" to be ruled by my conscience, I should stay with the Jew my master, who, God bless the mark, is a kind of devil; and, to run away from the Jew, I should be ruled by the fiend, who, saving your reverence, is the devil himself. Certainly the Jew is the very devil incarnal; and, in my conscience, my conscience is but a kind of hard conscience, to offer to counsel me to stay with the Jew. The fiend gives the more friendly counsel: I will run, fiend; my heels are at your command; I will run.

Enter Old GOBBO, *with a basket*

GOB.   Master young man, you, I pray you, which is the way to master Jew's?

LAUN.   [*Aside*] O heavens, this is my true-begotten father! who, being more than sand-blind, high-gravel blind,[1] knows me not: I will try confusions with him.

GOB.   Master young gentleman, I pray you, which is the way to master Jew's?

LAUN.   Turn up on your right hand at the next turning, but, at the next turning of all, on your left; marry, at the very next turning, turn of no hand, but turn down indirectly to the Jew's house.

GOB.   By God's sonties,[2] 't will be a hard way to hit. Can you tell me whether one Launcelot, that dwells with him, dwell with him or no?

LAUN.   Talk you of young Master Launcelot? [*Aside*] Mark me now; now will I raise the waters. Talk you of young Master Launcelot?

GOB.   No master, sir, but a poor man's son: his father, though I say it, is an honest exceeding poor man, and, God be thanked, well to live.

LAUN.   Well, let his father be what a' will, we talk of young Master Launcelot.

GOB.   Your worship's friend, and Launcelot, sir.

LAUN.   But I pray you, ergo, old man, ergo, I beseech you, talk you of young Master Launcelot?

GOB.   Of Launcelot, an 't please your mastership.

LAUN.   Ergo, Master Launcelot. Talk not of Master Launcelot, father; for the young gentleman, according to Fates and Destinies and such odd sayings, the Sisters Three and such branches of learning, is indeed deceased; or, as you would say in plain terms, gone to heaven.

GOB.   Marry, God forbid! the boy was the very staff of my age, my very prop.

LAUN.   Do I look like a cudgel or a hovel-post, a staff or a prop? Do you know me, father?

GOB.   Alack the day, I know you not, young gentleman: but, I pray you, tell me, is my boy, God rest his soul, alive or dead?

LAUN.   Do you not know me, father?

---

1. *sand-blind, high-gravel blind*] Launcelot here duplicates synonyms for "purblind." With "sand-blind" and "gravel-blind" compare "stone-blind," which was in common use for "completely blind."
2. *sonties*] Possibly old Gobbo's corruption of *santé* (health) or sanctity.

GOB.   Alack, sir, I am sand-blind; I know you not.

LAUN.   Nay, indeed, if you had your eyes, you might fail of the knowing me: it is a wise father that knows his own child. Well, old man, I will tell you news of your son: give me your blessing: truth will come to light; murder cannot be hid long; a man's son may; but, at the length, truth will out.

GOB.   Pray you, sir, stand up: I am sure you are not Launcelot, my boy.

LAUN.   Pray you, let 's have no more fooling about it, but give me your blessing: I am Launcelot, your boy that was, your son that is, your child that shall be.

GOB.   I cannot think you are my son.

LAUN.   I know not what I shall think of that: but I am Launcelot, the Jew's man; and I am sure Margery your wife is my mother.

GOB.   Her name is Margery, indeed: I 'll be sworn, if thou be Launcelot, thou art mine own flesh and blood. Lord worshipped might he be! what a beard[3] hast thou got! thou hast got more hair on thy chin than Dobbin my fill-horse has on his tail.

LAUN.   It should seem, then, that Dobbin's tail grows backward: I am sure he had more hair of his tail than I have of my face when I last saw him.

GOB.   Lord, how art thou changed! How dost thou and thy master agree? I have brought him a present. How 'gree you now?

LAUN.   Well, well: but, for my own part, as I have set up my rest to run away, so I will not rest till I have run some ground. My master 's a very Jew: give him a present! give him a halter: I am famished in his service; you may tell every finger I have with my ribs. Father, I am glad you are come: give me your present to one Master Bassanio, who, indeed, gives rare new liveries: if I serve not him, I will run as far as God has any ground. O rare fortune! here comes the man: to him, father; for I am a Jew, if I serve the Jew any longer.

Enter BASSANIO, *with* LEONARDO *and other followers*

BASS.   You may do so; but let it be so hasted, that supper be ready at the farthest by five of the clock. See these letters delivered; put the

---

3. *what a beard, etc.*] According to stage tradition, Launcelot kneels down with his back towards old Gobbo, who, touching the hair of his son's head, mistakes it for a beard.

liveries to making; and desire Gratiano to come anon to my lodging.   [*Exit a* Servant.]

LAUN.   To him, father.

GOB.   God bless your worship!

BASS.   Gramercy!⁴ wouldst thou aught with me?

GOB.   Here's my son, sir, a poor boy, —

LAUN.   Not a poor boy, sir, but the rich Jew's man; that would, sir, — as
my father shall specify, —

GOB.   He hath a great infection, sir, as one would say, to serve —

LAUN.   Indeed, the short and the long is, I serve the Jew, and have a
desire, — as my father shall specify, —

GOB.   His master and he, saving your worship's reverence, are scarce
cater-cousins, — ⁵

LAUN.   To be brief, the very truth is that the Jew, having done me
wrong, doth cause me, — as my father, being, I hope, an old man,
shall frutify⁶ unto you, —

GOB.   I have here a dish of doves that I would bestow upon your
worship, and my suit is, —

LAUN.   In very brief, the suit is impertinent to myself, as your worship
shall know by this honest old man; and, though I say it, though old
man, yet poor man, my father.

BASS.   One speak for both. What would you?

LAUN.   Serve you, sir.

GOB.   That is the very defect of the matter, sir.

BASS.   I know thee well; thou hast obtain'd thy suit:
Shylock thy master spoke with me this day,
And hath preferr'd thee, if it be preferment
To leave a rich Jew's service, to become
The follower of so poor a gentleman.

LAUN.   The old proverb is very well parted between my master Shylock

---

4. *Gramercy!*] Great thanks!

5. *cater-cousins*] quatre-cousins, remote relations. Old Gobbo misapplies the term here to
mean persons who peaceably eat together.

6. *frutify*] used by Launcelot for "notify."

and you, sir: you have the grace of God, sir, and he hath enough.

BASS.   Thou speak'st it well. Go, father, with thy son.

Take leave of thy old master and inquire

My lodging out. Give him a livery

More guarded[7] than his fellows': see it done.

LAUN.   Father, in. I cannot get a service, no; I have ne'er a tongue in
my head. Well, if any man in Italy have a fairer table[8] which doth
offer to swear upon a book,[9] I shall have good fortune. Go to, here's
a simple line of life: here's a small trifle of wives: alas, fifteen wives
is nothing! a 'leven widows and nine maids is a simple coming-in
for one man: and then to 'scape drowning thrice, and to be in peril
of my life with the edge of a feather-bed; here are simple scapes.
Well, if Fortune be a woman, she's a good wench for this gear.
Father, come; I'll take my leave of the Jew in the twinkling of
an eye.   [Exeunt LAUNCELOT and Old GOBBO.]

BASS.   I pray thee, good Leonardo, think on this:

These things being bought and orderly bestow'd,

Return in haste, for I do feast to-night

My best-esteem'd acquaintance: hie thee, go.

LEON.   My best endeavours shall be done herein.

Enter GRATIANO

GRA.   Where is your master?

LEON.   Yonder, sir, he walks.   [*Exit.*]

GRA.   Signior Bassanio, —

BASS.   Gratiano!

GRA.   I have a suit to you.

BASS.   You have obtain'd it.

GRA.   You must not deny me: I must go with you to Belmont.

---

7. *More guarded*] Better trimmed, ornamented with more lace or gold braid, which
usually edged a garment and "guarded" it from fraying.

8. *table*] The speaker is here looking at the palm of his hand, which in palmistry was
technically known as the "table."

9. *which doth offer . . . book*] which gives positive assurance. To "swear upon a book" is to
take an oath of the most binding force.

BASS.   Why, then you must. But hear thee, Gratiano:
    Thou art too wild, too rude, and bold of voice;
    Parts that become thee happily enough,
    And in such eyes as ours appear not faults;
    But where thou art not known, why there they show
    Something too liberal. Pray thee, take pain
    To allay with some cold drops of modesty
    Thy skipping spirit; lest, through thy wild behaviour,
    I be misconstrued in the place I go to,
    And lose my hopes.

GRA.   Signior Bassanio, hear me:
    If I do not put on a sober habit,
    Talk with respect, and swear but now and then,
    Wear prayer-books in my pocket, look demurely;
    Nay more, while grace is saying, hood mine eyes
    Thus with my hat, and sigh, and say "amen;"
    Use all the observance of civility,
    Like one well studied in a sad ostent[10]
    To please his grandam, never trust me more.

BASS.   Well, we shall see your bearing.

GRA.   Nay, but I bar to-night: you shall not gauge me
    By what we do to-night.

BASS.   No, that were pity:
    I would entreat you rather to put on
    Your boldest suit of mirth, for we have friends
    That purpose merriment. But fare you well:
    I have some business.

GRA.   And I must to Lorenzo and the rest:
    But we will visit you at supper-time.   [*Exeunt.*]

---

10. *sad ostent*] serious aspect or demeanor.

·SCENE III. *The same. A room in* SHYLOCK'S *house.*

Enter JESSICA *and* LAUNCELOT

JES.   I am sorry thou wilt leave my father so:
      Our house is hell; and thou, a merry devil,
      Didst rob it of some taste of tediousness.
      But fare thee well; there is a ducat for thee:
      And, Launcelot, soon at supper shalt thou see
      Lorenzo, who is thy new master's guest:
      Give him this letter; do it secretly;
      And so farewell: I would not have my father
      See me in talk with thee.
LAUN.   Adieu! tears exhibit my tongue.[1] Most beautiful pagan, most
      sweet Jew! if a Christian did not play the knave, and get[2] thee, I am
      much deceived. But, adieu: these foolish drops do something
      drown my manly spirit: adieu.
JES.   Farewell, good Launcelot.   [*Exit* LAUNCELOT.]
      Alack, what heinous sin is it in me
      To be ashamed to be my father's child!
      But though I am a daughter to his blood,
      I am not to his manners. O Lorenzo,
      If thou keep promise, I shall end this strife,
      Become a Christian, and thy loving wife.   [*Exit.*]

---

1. *exhibit my tongue*] show what my tongue ought to express.
2. *get*] beget.

SCENE IV. *The same. A street.*

Enter GRATIANO, LORENZO, SALARINO, *and* SALANIO

LOR.   Nay, we will slink away in supper-time,
    Disguise us at my lodging, and return
    All in an hour.
GRA.   We have not made good preparation.
SALAR.   We have not spoke us yet of torch-bearers.
SALAN.   'T is vile, unless it may be quaintly order'd,[1]
    And better in my mind not undertook.
LOR.   'T is now but four o'clock: we have two hours
    To furnish us.

Enter LAUNCELOT *with a letter*

            Friend Launcelot, what 's the news?
LAUN.   An it shall please you to break up this, it shall seem to signify.
LOR.   I know the hand: in faith, 't is a fair hand;
    And whiter than the paper it writ on
    Is the fair hand that writ.
GRA.   Love-news, in faith.
LAUN.   By your leave, sir.
LOR.   Whither goest thou?
LAUN.   Marry, sir, to bid my old master the Jew to sup to-night with my
new master the Christian.
LOR.   Hold here, take this: tell gentle Jessica
    I will not fail her; speak it privately.
    Go, gentlemen,   [*Exit* LAUNCELOT.]
    Will you prepare you for this masque to-night?
    I am provided of a torch-bearer.
SALAR.   Ay, marry, I 'll be gone about it straight.
SALAN.   And so will I.

---

1. *quaintly order'd*] ingeniously, cleverly arranged.

LOR.   Meet me and Gratiano
    At Gratiano's lodging some hour hence.
SALAR. 'T is good we do so.   [*Exeunt* SALARINO *and* SALANIO.]
GRA.   Was not that letter from fair Jessica?
LOR.   I must needs tell thee all. She hath directed
    How I shall take her from her father's house;
    What gold and jewels she is furnish'd with;
    What page's suit she hath in readiness.
    If e'er the Jew her father come to heaven,
    It will be for his gentle daughter's sake:
    And never dare misfortune cross her foot,
    Unless she do it under this excuse,
    That she is issue to a faithless Jew.
    Come, go with me; peruse this as thou goest:
    Fair Jessica shall be my torch-bearer.   [*Exeunt.*]

SCENE V. *The same. Before* SHYLOCK'S *house.*

Enter SHYLOCK *and* LAUNCELOT

SHY.   Well, thou shalt see, thy eyes shall be thy judge,
    The difference of old Shylock and Bassanio: —
    What, Jessica! — thou shalt not gormandise,
    As thou hast done with me: — What, Jessica! —
    And sleep and snore, and rend apparel out; —
    Why, Jessica, I say!
LAUN.   Why, Jessica!
SHY.   Who bids thee call? I do not bid thee call.
LAUN.   Your worship was wont to tell me that I could do nothing
    without bidding.

Enter JESSICA

JES.   Call you? what is your will?

SHY.   I am bid forth to supper, Jessica:
        There are my keys. But wherefore should I go?
        I am not bid for love; they flatter me:
        But yet I 'll go in hate, to feed upon
        The prodigal Christian. Jessica, my girl,
        Look to my house. I am right loath to go:
        There is some ill a-brewing towards my rest,
        For I did dream of money-bags to-night.
LAUN.   I beseech you, sir, go: my young master doth expect your
        reproach.
SHY.   So do I his.
LAUN.   And they have conspired together, I will not say you shall see a
        masque; but if you do, then it was not for nothing that my nose fell
        a-bleeding on Black-Monday last at six o'clock i' the morning,
        falling out that year on Ash-Wednesday was four year, in the
        afternoon.
SHY.   What, are there masques? Hear you me, Jessica:
        Lock up my doors; and when you hear the drum,
        And the vile squealing of the wry-neck'd fife,
        Clamber not you up to the casements then,
        Nor thrust your head into the public street
        To gaze on Christian fools with varnish'd faces;
        But stop my house's ears, I mean my casements:
        Let not the sound of shallow foppery enter
        My sober house. By Jacob's staff, I swear
        I have no mind of feasting forth to-night:
        But I will go. Go you before me, sirrah;
        Say I will come.
LAUN.   I will go before, sir. Mistress, look out at window, for all this;

                There will come a Christian by,
                Will be worth a Jewess' eye.   [*Exit.*]

SHY.   What says that fool of Hagar's offspring, ha?
JES.   His words were, "Farewell, mistress;" nothing else.
SHY.   The patch[1] is kind enough, but a huge feeder;

---

1. *patch*] a paltry fellow, interpreted in this passage as a domestic fool, called "patch"
because of his parti-colored dress.

Snail-slow in profit, and he sleeps by day
More than the wild-cat: drones hive not with me;
Therefore I part with him; and part with him
To one that I would have him help to waste
His borrow'd purse. Well, Jessica, go in:
Perhaps I will return immediately:
Do as I bid you; shut doors after you:
Fast bind, fast find,
A proverb never stale in thrifty mind.   [*Exit.*]
JES.   Farewell; and if my fortune be not crost,
I have a father, you a daughter, lost.   [*Exit.*]

SCENE VI. *The same.*

Enter GRATIANO *and* SALARINO, *masqued*

GRA.   This is the pent-house under which Lorenzo
    Desired us to make stand.
SALAR.   His hour is almost past.
GRA.   And it is marvel he out-dwells his hour,
    For lovers ever run before the clock.
SALAR.   O, ten times faster Venus' pigeons fly
    To seal love's bonds new-made, than they are wont
    To keep obliged faith unforfeited!
GRA.   That ever holds: who riseth from a feast
    With that keen appetite that he sits down?
    Where is the horse that doth untread again
    His tedious measures with the unbated fire
    That he did pace them first? All things that are,
    Are with more spirit chased than enjoy'd.
    How like a younker[1] or a prodigal

---

1. *younker*] a stripling.

The scarfed bark puts from her native bay,
Hugg'd and embraced by the strumpet wind!
How like the prodigal doth she return,
With over-weather'd ribs and ragged sails,
Lean, rent, and beggar'd by the strumpet wind!

SALAR.   Here comes Lorenzo: more of this hereafter.

Enter LORENZO

LOR.   Sweet friends, your patience for my long abode;
Not I, but my affairs, have made you wait:
When you shall please to play the thieves for wives,
I 'll watch as long for you then. Approach;
Here dwells my father Jew. Ho! who 's within?

Enter JESSICA, *above, in boy's clothes*

JES.   Who are you? Tell me, for more certainty,
Albeit I 'll swear that I do know your tongue.

LOR.   Lorenzo, and thy love.

JÉS.   Lorenzo, certain; and my love, indeed,
For who love I so much? And now who knows
But you, Lorenzo, whether I am yours?

LOR.   Heaven and thy thoughts are witness that thou art.

JES.   Here, catch this casket; it is worth the pains.
I am glad 't is night, you do not look on me,
For I am much ashamed of my exchange:
But love is blind, and lovers cannot see
The pretty follies that themselves commit;
For if they could, Cupid himself would blush
To see me thus transformed to a boy.

LOR.   Descend, for you must be my torch-bearer.

JES.   What, must I hold a candle to my shames?
They in themselves, good sooth, are too too light.
Why, 't is an office of discovery, love;
And I should be obscured.

LOR.   So are you, sweet,
Even in the lovely garnish[2] of a boy.

---

2. *garnish*] outfit or dress.

But come at once;
For the close night doth play the runaway,
And we are stay'd for at Bassanio's feast.

JES.   I will make fast the doors, and gild myself
With some mo ducats, and be with you straight.   [*Exit above.*]

GRA.   Now, by my hood,[3] a Gentile, and no Jew.

LOR.   Beshrew me[4] but I love her heartily;
For she is wise, if I can judge of her;
And fair she is, if that mine eyes be true;
And true she is, as she hath proved herself;
And therefore, like herself, wise, fair, and true,
Shall she be placed in my constant soul.

Enter JESSICA, *below*

What, art thou come? On, gentlemen; away!
Our masquing mates by this time for us stay.

[*Exit with* JESSICA *and* SALARINO.]

Enter ANTONIO

ANT.   Who 's there?

GRA.   Signior Antonio!

ANT.   Fie, fie, Gratiano; where are all the rest?
'T is nine o'clock: our friends all stay for you.
No masque to-night: the wind is come about;
Bassanio presently will go aboard:
I have sent twenty out to seek for you.

GRA.   I am glad on 't: I desire no more delight
Than to be under sail and gone to-night.   [*Exeunt.*]

---

3. *by my hood*] An expletive objurgation, which may have originally been employed by
hooded monks or friars.
4. *Beshrew me*] A simple assertion, such as "Indeed."

Scene VII. *Belmont.* A room in Portia's *house.*

Flourish of cornets. Enter Portia, *with the* Prince of Morocco, *and their trains*

Por.   Go draw aside the curtains, and discover[1]
    The several caskets to this noble prince.
    Now make your choice.
Mor.   The first, of gold, who this inscription bears,
    "Who chooseth me shall gain what many men desire;"
    The second, silver, which this promise carries,
    "Who chooseth me shall get as much as he deserves;"
    This third, dull lead, with warning all as blunt,
    "Who chooseth me must give and hazard all he hath."
    How shall I know if I do choose the right?
Por.   The one of them contains my picture, prince:
    If you choose that, then I am yours withal.
Mor.   Some god direct my judgement! Let me see;
    I will survey the inscriptions back again.
    What says this leaden casket?
    "Who chooseth me must give and hazard all he hath."
    Must give, — for what? for lead? hazard for lead?
    This casket threatens. Men that hazard all
    Do it in hope of fair advantages:
    A golden mind stoops not to shows of dross;
    I 'll then nor give nor hazard aught for lead.
    What says the silver with her virgin hue?
    "Who chooseth me shall get as much as he deserves."
    As much as he deserves! Pause there, Morocco,
    And weigh thy value with an even hand:
    If thou be'st rated by thy estimation,
    Thou dost deserve enough; and yet enough

---

1. *discover*] reveal.

May not extend so far as to the lady:
And yet to be afeard of my deserving
Were but a weak disabling of myself.
As much as I deserve! Why, that 's the lady:
I do in birth deserve her, and in fortunes,
In graces and in qualities of breeding;
But more than these, in love I do deserve.
What if I stray'd no further, but chose here?
Let 's see once more this saying graved in gold;
"Who chooseth me shall gain what many men desire."
Why, that 's the lady; all the world desires her;
From the four corners of the earth they come,
To kiss this shrine, this mortal-breathing saint:
The Hyrcanian deserts[2] and the vasty wilds
Of wide Arabia are as throughfares now
For princes to come view fair Portia:
The watery kingdom, whose ambitious head
Spits in the face of heaven, is no bar
To stop the foreign spirits; but they come,
As o'er a brook, to see fair Portia.
One of these three contains her heavenly picture.
Is 't like that lead contains her? 'T were damnation
To think so base a thought: it were too gross
To rib her cerecloth[3] in the obscure grave.
Or shall I think in silver she 's immured,
Being ten times undervalued to tried gold?
O sinful thought! Never so rich a gem
Was set in worse than gold. They have in England
A coin that bears the figure of an angel[4]
Stamped in gold, but that 's insculp'd upon;
But here an angel in a golden bed

---

2. *Hyrcanian deserts*] wild tracts to the southeast of the Caspian Sea where tigers were reputed to abound.
3. *rib her cerecloth*] enclose, encircle (like ribs) her winding sheet.
4. *angel*] A gold coin worth about ten shillings, on one side of which was stamped in high relief a figure of the archangel Michael.

Lies all within. Deliver me the key:
Here do I choose, and thrive I as I may!

POR.   There, take it, prince; and if my form lie there,
Then I am yours.   [*He unlocks the golden casket.*]

MOR.   O hell! what have we here?
A carrion Death, within whose empty eye
There is a written scroll! I 'll read the writing.   [*Reads.*]

> All that glisters is not gold;
> Often have you heard that told:
> Many a man his life hath sold
> But my outside to behold:
> Gilded tombs do worms infold.
> Had you been as wise as bold,
> Young in limbs, in judgement old,
> Your answer had not been inscroll'd:
> Fare you well; your suit is cold.

Cold, indeed and labour lost:
Then, farewell, heat, and welcome, frost!
Portia, adieu. I have too grieved a heart
To take a tedious leave: thus losers part.
                    [*Exit with his train. Flourish of cornets.*]

POR.   A gentle riddance. Draw the curtains, go.
Let all of his complexion choose me so.   [*Exeunt.*]

SCENE VIII. *Venice. A street.*

Enter SALARINO *and* SALANIO

SALAR.   Why, man, I saw Bassanio under sail:
With him is Gratiano gone along;
And in their ship I am sure Lorenzo is not.

SALAN.   The villain Jew with outcries raised the Duke,
Who went with him to search Bassanio's ship.

SALAR.   He came too late, the ship was under sail:

But there the Duke was given to understand
That in a gondola were seen together
Lorenzo and his amorous Jessica:
Besides, Antonio certified the Duke
They were not with Bassanio in his ship.

SALAN.   I never heard a passion so confused,
So strange, outrageous, and so variable,
As the dog Jew did utter in the streets:
"My daughter! O my ducats! O my daughter!
Fled with a Christian! O my Christian ducats!
Justice! the law! my ducats, and my daughter!
A sealed bag, two sealed bags of ducats,
Of double ducats, stolen from me by my daughter!
And jewels, two stones, two rich and precious stones,
Stolen by my daughter! Justice! find the girl!
She hath the stones upon her, and the ducats!"

SALAR.   Why, all the boys in Venice follow him,
Crying, his stones, his daughter, and his ducats.

SALAN.   Let good Antonio look he keep his day,
Or he shall pay for this.

SALAR.   Marry, well remember'd.
I reason'd with a Frenchman yesterday,
Who told me, in the narrow seas that part
The French and English, there miscarried
A vessel of our country richly fraught:
I thought upon Antonio when he told me;
And wish'd in silence that it were not his.

SALAN.   You were best to tell Antonio what you hear;
Yet do not suddenly, for it may grieve him.

SALAR.   A kinder gentleman treads not the earth.
I saw Bassanio and Antonio part:
Bassanio told him he would make some speed
Of his return: he answer'd, "Do not so;
Slubber[1] not business for my sake, Bassanio,
But stay the very riping of the time;

---

1. *Slubber*] To do carelessly or negligently.

And for the Jew's bond which he hath of me,
Let it not enter in your mind of love:
Be merry; and employ your chiefest thoughts
To courtship, and such fair ostents[2] of love
As shall conveniently become you there:"
And even there, his eye being big with tears,
Turning his face, he put his hand behind him,
And with affection wondrous sensible
He wrung Bassanio's hand; and so they parted.

SALAN.   I think he only loves the world for him.
I pray thee, let us go and find him out,
And quicken his embraced heaviness
With some delight or other.

SALAR.   Do we so.   [*Exeunt.*]

SCENE IX. *Belmont. A room in* PORTIA'S *house.*

Enter NERISSA *and a* Servitor

NER.   Quick, quick, I pray thee: draw the curtain straight:
The Prince of Arragon hath ta'en his oath,
And comes to his election presently.

Flourish of cornets. Enter the PRINCE OF ARRAGON, PORTIA, *and their trains*

POR.   Behold, there stand the caskets, noble prince:
If you choose that wherein I am contain'd,
Straight shall our nuptial rites be solemnized:
But if you fail, without more speech, my lord,
You must be gone from hence immediately.

AR.   I am enjoin'd by oath to observe three things:
First, never to unfold to any one

---

2. *ostents*] external shows.

Which casket 't was I chose; next, if I fail
Of the right casket, never in my life
To woo a maid in way of marriage:
Lastly,
If I do fail in fortune of my choice,
Immediately to leave you and be gone.

POR.   To these injunctions every one doth swear
That comes to hazard for my worthless self.

AR.   And so have I address'd me. Fortune now
To my heart's hope! Gold; silver; and base lead.
"Who chooseth me must give and hazard all he hath."
You shall look fairer, ere I give or hazard.
What says the golden chest? ha! let me see:
"Who chooseth me shall gain what many men desire."
What many men desire! that "many" may be meant
By the fool multitude, that choose by show,
Not learning more than the fond eye doth teach;
Which pries not to the interior, but, like the martlet,[1]
Builds in the weather on the outward wall,
Even in the force and road of casualty.
I will not choose what many men desire,
Because I will not jump with common spirits,
And rank me with the barbarous multitudes.
Why, then to thee, thou silver treasure-house;
Tell me once more what title thou dost bear:
"Who chooseth me shall get as much as he deserves:"
And well said too; for who shall go about
To cozen[2] fortune, and be honourable
Without the stamp of merit? Let none presume
To wear an undeserved dignity.
O, that estates, degrees and offices
Were not derived corruptly, and that clear honour
Were purchased by the merit of the wearer!
How many then should cover that stand bare!

---

1. *martlet*] Used here for the "house martin," but more properly the swift.
2. *cozen*] cheat.

How many be commanded that command!
How much low peasantry would then be glean'd
From the true seed of honour![3] and how much honour
Pick'd from the chaff and ruin of the times,
To be new-varnish'd! Well, but to my choice:
"Who chooseth me shall get as much as he deserves."
I will assume desert. Give me a key for this,
And instantly unlock my fortunes here.

[*He opens the silver casket.*]

POR.   [*Aside*] Too long a pause for that which you find there.

AR.   What's here? the portrait of a blinking idiot,
Presenting me a schedule! I will read it.
How much unlike art thou to Portia!
How much unlike my hopes and my deservings!
"Who chooseth me shall have as much as he deserves."
Did I deserve no more than a fool's head?
Is that my prize? are my deserts no better?

POR.   To offend, and judge, are distinct offices,
And of opposed natures.

AR.   What is here?

[*Reads*]   The fire seven times tried this:
                   Seven times tried that judgement is,
                   That did never choose amiss.
                   Some there be that shadows kiss;
                   Such have but a shadow's bliss:
                   There be fools alive, I wis,
                   Silver'd o'er; and so was this.
                   Take what wife you will to bed,
                   I will ever be your head:
                   So be gone: you are sped.

          Still more fool I shall appear
          By the time I linger here:

---

3. *How much low peasantry . . . honour!*] How much vulgarity or boorishness would then
be detected in those succeeding to high office by hereditary right.

      With one fool's head I came to woo,
      But I go away with two.
      Sweet, adieu. I 'll keep my oath,
      Patiently to bear my wroth.

                       [*Exeunt* ARRAGON *and train.*]

POR.   Thus hath the candle singed the moth.
      O, these deliberate fools! when they do choose,
      They have the wisdom by their wit to lose.
NER.   The ancient saying is no heresy,
      Hanging and wiving goes by destiny.
POR.   Come, draw the curtain, Nerissa.

Enter a Servant

SERV.   Where is my lady?
POR.   Here: what would my lord?
SERV.   Madam, there is alighted at your gate
      A young Venetian, one that comes before
      To signify the approaching of his lord;
      From whom he bringeth sensible regreets,[4]
      To wit, besides commends and courteous breath,
      Gifts of rich value. Yet I have not seen
      So likely an ambassador of love:
      A day in April never came so sweet,
      To show how costly summer was at hand,
      As this fore-spurrer comes before his lord.
POR.   No more, I pray thee: I am half afeard
      Thou wilt say anon he is some kin to thee,
      Thou spend'st such high-day wit[5] in praising him.
      Come, come, Nerissa; for I long to see
      Quick Cupid's post that comes so mannerly.
NER.   Bassanio, lord Love, if thy will it be!   [*Exeunt.*]

---

4. *regreets*] greetings.
5. *high-day wit*] holiday, cheerful wit.

ACT III

SCENE I. *Venice. A street.*

Enter SALANIO *and* SALARINO

SALAN. Now, what news on the Rialto?

SALAR. Why, yet it lives there unchecked, that Antonio hath a ship of rich lading wrecked on the narrow seas; the Goodwins, I think they call the place; a very dangerous flat and fatal, where the carcases of many a tall ship lie buried, as they say, if my gossip Report be an honest woman of her word.

SALAN. I would she were as lying a gossip in that as ever knapped ginger,[1] or made her neighbours believe she wept for the death of a third husband. But it is true, without any slips of prolixity, or crossing the plain highway of talk, that the good Antonio, the honest Antonio,—O that I had a title good enough to keep his name company!—

SALAR. Come, the full stop.

SALAN. Ha! what sayest thou? Why, the end is, he hath lost a ship.

SALAR. I would it might prove the end of his losses.

SALAN. Let me say "amen" betimes, lest the devil cross my prayer, for here he comes in the likeness of a Jew.

Enter SHYLOCK

How now, Shylock! what news among the merchants?

---

1. *knapped ginger*] gnawed or nibbled off ginger. A taste for ginger was commonly held at the time to be characteristic of old women.

SHY. You knew, none so well, none so well as you, of my daughter's flight.

SALAR. That 's certain: I, for my part, knew the tailor that made the wings she flew withal.

SALAN. And Shylock, for his own part, knew the bird was fledged; and then it is the complexion of them all to leave the dam.

SHY. She is damned for it.

SALAR. That 's certain, if the devil may be her judge.

SHY. My own flesh and blood to rebel!

SALAN. Out upon it, old carrion! rebels it at these years?

SHY. I say, my daughter is my flesh and blood.

SALAR. There is more difference between thy flesh and hers than between jet and ivory; more between your bloods than there is between red wine and rhenish. But tell us, do you hear whether Antonio have had any loss at sea or no?

SHY. There I have another bad match: a bankrupt, a prodigal, who dare scarce show his head on the Rialto; a beggar, that was used to come so smug upon the mart; let him look to his bond: he was wont to call me usurer; let him look to his bond: he was wont to lend money for a Christian courtesy; let him look to his bond.

SALAR. Why, I am sure, if he forfeit, thou wilt not take his flesh: what 's that good for?

SHY. To bait fish withal: if it will feed nothing else, it will feed my revenge. He hath disgraced me, and hindered me half a million; laughed at my losses, mocked at my gains, scorned my nation, thwarted my bargains, cooled my friends, heated mine enemies; and what 's his reason? I am a Jew. Hath not a Jew eyes? hath not a Jew hands, organs, dimensions, senses, affections, passions? fed with the same food, hurt with the same weapons, subject to the same diseases, healed by the same means, warmed and cooled by the same winter and summer, as a Christian is? If you prick us, do we not bleed? if you tickle us, do we not laugh? if you poison us, do we not die? and if you wrong us, shall we not revenge? if we are like you in the rest, we will resemble you in that. If a Jew wrong a Christian, what is his humility?[2] Revenge. If a Christian wrong a

---

2. *humility*] humanity, benevolence, kindness, not "humbleness."

Jew, what should his sufferance be by Christian example? Why, revenge. The villany you teach me, I will execute; and it shall go hard but I will better the instruction.

Enter a Servant

SERV.   Gentlemen, my master Antonio is at his house, and desires to speak with you both.

SALAR.   We have been up and down to seek him.

Enter TUBAL

SALAN.   Here comes another of the tribe: a third cannot be matched, unless the devil himself turn Jew.

[*Exeunt* SALANIO, SALARINO, *and* Servant.]

SHY.   How now, Tubal! what news from Genoa? hast thou found my daughter?

TUB.   I often came where I did hear of her, but cannot find her.

SHY.   Why, there, there, there, there! a diamond gone, cost me two thousand ducats in Frankfort! The curse never fell upon our nation till now; I never felt it till now: two thousand ducats in that; and other precious, precious jewels. I would my daughter were dead at my foot, and the jewels in her ear! would she were hearsed at my foot, and the ducats in her coffin! No news of them? Why, so: — and I know not what's spent in the search: why, thou loss upon loss! the thief gone with so much, and so much to find the thief; and no satisfaction, no revenge: nor no ill luck stirring but what lights on my shoulders; no sighs but of my breathing; no tears but of my shedding.

TUB.   Yes, other men have ill luck too: Antonio, as I heard in Genoa, —

SHY.   What, what, what? ill luck, ill luck?

TUB.   Hath an argosy³ cast away, coming from Tripolis.

SHY.   I thank God, I thank God! Is 't true, is 't true?

TUB.   I spoke with some of the sailors that escaped the wreck.

SHY.   I thank thee, good Tubal: good news, good news! ha, ha! where? in Genoa?

---

3. *argosy*] large merchantman.

TUB. Your daughter spent in Genoa, as I heard, in one night fourscore ducats.

SHY. Thou stick'st a dagger in me: I shall never see my gold again: fourscore ducats at a sitting! fourscore ducats!

TUB. There came divers[4] of Antonio's creditors in my company to Venice, that swear he cannot choose but break.

SHY. I am very glad of it: I 'll plague him; I 'll torture him: I am glad of it.

TUB. One of them showed me a ring that he had of your daughter for a monkey.

SHY. Out upon her! Thou torturest me, Tubal: it was my turquoise; I had it of Leah[5] when I was a bachelor: I would not have given it for a wilderness of monkeys.

TUB. But Antonio is certainly undone.

SHY. Nay, that 's true, that 's very true. Go, Tubal, fee me an officer; bespeak him a fortnight before. I will have the heart of him, if he forfeit; for, were he out of Venice, I can make what merchandise I will. Go, go, Tubal, and meet me at our synagogue; go, good Tubal; at our synagogue, Tubal.   [*Exeunt.*]

SCENE II. *Belmont.* A room in PORTIA'S *house.*

Enter BASSANIO, PORTIA, GRATIANO, NERISSA, *and* Attendants

POR. I pray you, tarry: pause a day or two
      Before you hazard; for, in choosing wrong,
      I lose your company: therefore forbear awhile.
      There 's something tells me, but it is not love,
      I would not lose you; and you know yourself,

---

4. *divers*] several, sundry.
5. *I had it of Leah*] Shylock received the ring from his dead wife Leah.

Hate counsels not in such a quality.
But lest you should not understand me well, —
And yet a maiden hath no tongue but thought,[1] —
I would detain you here some month or two
Before you venture for me. I could teach you
How to choose right, but I am then forsworn;
So will I never be: so may you miss me;
But if you do, you 'll make me wish a sin,
That I had been forsworn. Beshrew your eyes,
They have o'er-look'd me, and divided me;
One half of me is yours, the other half yours,
Mine own, I would say; but if mine, then yours,
And so all yours! O, these naughty times
Put bars between the owners and their rights!
And so, though yours, not yours. Prove it so,
Let fortune go to hell for it, not I.
I speak too long; but 't is to peize[2] the time,
To eke it and to draw it out in length,
To stay you from election.

BASS.   Let me choose;
  For as I am, I live upon the rack.

POR.   Upon the rack, Bassanio! then confess
  What treason there is mingled with your love.

BASS.   None but that ugly treason of mistrust,
  Which makes me fear the enjoying of my love:
  There may as well be amity and life
  'Tween snow and fire, as treason and my love.

POR.   Ay, but I fear you speak upon the rack,
  Where men enforced do speak any thing.

BASS.   Promise me life, and I 'll confess the truth.

POR.   Well then, confess and live.

BASS.   "Confess," and "love,"

---

1. *a maiden ... thought*] a maiden is restrained by modesty from giving expression to her love, and must only cherish it in thought.
2. *to peize*] to poise; here, to retard time by hanging weights on it.

Had been the very sum of my confession:
O happy torment, when my torturer
Doth teach me answers for deliverance!
But let me to my fortune and the caskets.

POR.   Away, then! I am lock'd in one of them:
If you do love me, you will find me out.
Nerissa and the rest, stand all aloof.
Let music sound while he doth make his choice;
Then, if he lose, he makes a swan-like end,
Fading in music: that the comparison
May stand more proper, my eye shall be the stream,
And watery death-bed for him. He may win;
And what is music then? Then music is
Even as the flourish when true subjects bow
To a new-crowned monarch: such it is
As are those dulcet sounds in break of day
That creep into the dreaming bridegroom's ear,
And summon him to marriage. Now he goes,
With no less presence, but with much more love,
Than young Alcides,[3] when he did redeem
The virgin tribute paid by howling Troy
To the sea-monster: I stand for sacrifice;
The rest aloof are the Dardanian[4] wives,
With bleared visages, come forth to view
The issue of the exploit. Go, Hercules!
Live thou, I live: with much much more dismay
I view the fight than thou that makest the fray.

---

3. *young Alcides*] Ovid tells the story, in *Metamorphoses*, XI, how Hercules rescued from
   the sea monster the Trojan maiden Hesione, who had been sacrificed to free the town
   of Troy from pestilence, not for love of her, but on condition of receiving a gift of horses,
   from the girl's father, Laomedon.
4. *Dardanian*] Trojan.

Music, whilst BASSANIO *comments on the caskets to himself*

SONG

Tell me where is fancy bred,
Or in the heart or in the head?
How begot, how nourished?
        Reply, reply.
It is engender'd in the eyes,
With gazing fed; and fancy dies
In the cradle where it lies.
        Let us all ring fancy's knell;
        I 'll begin it, — Ding, dong, bell.

ALL.   Ding, dong, bell.

BASS.   So may the outward shows be least themselves:
The world is still deceived with ornament.
In law, what plea so tainted and corrupt,
But, being season'd with a gracious voice,
Obscures the show of evil? In religion,
What damned error, but some sober brow
Will bless it, and approve it with a text,
Hiding the grossness with fair ornament?
There is no vice so simple, but assumes
Some mark of virtue on his outward parts:
How many cowards, whose hearts are all as false
As stairs of sand, wear yet upon their chins
The beards of Hercules and frowning Mars;
Who, inward search'd, have livers white as milk;
And these assume but valour's excrement
To render them redoubted! Look on beauty,
And you shall see 't is purchased by the weight;
Which therein works a miracle in nature,
Making them lightest that wear most of it:
So are those crisped snaky golden locks
Which make such wanton gambols with the wind,
Upon supposed fairness, often known

To be the dowry of a second head,[5]
The skull that bred them in the sepulchre.
Thus ornament is but the guiled shore
To a most dangerous sea; the beauteous scarf
Veiling an Indian beauty; in a word,
The seeming truth which cunning times put on
To entrap the wisest. Therefore, thou gaudy gold,
Hard food for Midas, I will none of thee;
Nor none of thee, thou pale and common drudge
'Tween man and man: but thou, thou meagre lead,
Which rather threatenest than dost promise aught,
Thy paleness moves me more than eloquence;
And here choose I: joy be the consequence!

POR. [*Aside*] How all the other passions fleet to air,
As doubtful thoughts, and rash-embraced despair,
And shuddering fear, and green-eyed jealousy!
O love, be moderate; allay thy ecstasy;
In measure rain thy joy; scant this excess!
I feel too much thy blessing: make it less,
For fear I surfeit!

BASS.   What find I here? [*Opening the leaden casket.*]
Fair Portia's counterfeit! What demi-god
Hath come so near creation? Move these eyes?
Or whether, riding on the balls of mine,
Seem they in motion? Here are sever'd lips,
Parted with sugar breath: so sweet a bar
Should sunder such sweet friends. Here in her hairs
The painter plays the spider, and hath woven
A golden mesh to entrap the hearts of men,
Faster than gnats in cobwebs: but her eyes, —
How could he see to do them? having made one,
Methinks it should have power to steal both his
And leave itself unfurnish'd. Yet look, how far
The substance of my praise doth wrong this shadow

---

5. *a second head*] It was a common practice to wear false hair or hair cut from the heads of corpses.

In underprizing it, so far this shadow
Doth limp behind the substance. Here 's the scroll,
The continent and summary of my fortune.

> [*Reads*]   You that choose not by the view,
> Chance as fair, and choose as true!
> Since this fortune falls to you,
> Be content and seek no new.
> If you be well pleased with this,
> And hold your fortune for your bliss,
> Turn you where your lady is,
> And claim her with a loving kiss.

A gentle scroll. Fair lady, by your leave;
I come by note, to give and to receive.
Like one of two contending in a prize,
That thinks he hath done well in people's eyes,
Hearing applause and universal shout,
Giddy in spirit, still gazing in a doubt
Whether those peals of praise be his or no;
So, thrice-fair lady, stand I, even so;
As doubtful whether what I see be true,
Until confirm'd, sign'd, ratified by you.

POR.   You see me, Lord Bassanio, where I stand,
Such as I am: though for myself alone
I would not be ambitious in my wish,
To wish myself much better; yet, for you
I would be treble twenty times myself;
A thousand times more fair, ten thousand times
More rich;
That only to stand high in your account,
I might in virtues, beauties, livings, friends,
Exceed account; but the full sum of me
Is sum of something, which, to term in gross,
Is an unlesson'd girl, unschool'd, unpractised;
Happy in this, she is not yet so old
But she may learn; happier than this,
She is not bred so dull but she can learn;
Happiest of all is that her gentle spirit

Commits itself to yours to be directed,
As from her lord, her governor, her king.
Myself and what is mine to you and yours
Is now converted: but now I was the lord
Of this fair mansion, master of my servants,
Queen o'er myself; and even now, but now,
This house, these servants, and this same myself,
Are yours, my lord: I give them with this ring;
Which when you part from, lose, or give away,
Let it presage the ruin of your love,
And be my vantage to exclaim on you.

BASS. Madam, you have bereft me of all words,
Only my blood speaks to you in my veins;
And there is such confusion in my powers,
As, after some oration fairly spoke
By a beloved prince, there doth appear
Among the buzzing pleased multitude;
Where every something, being blent together,
Turns to a wild of nothing, save of joy,
Express'd and not express'd. But when this ring
Parts from this finger, then parts life from hence:
O, then be bold to say Bassanio 's dead!

NER. My lord and lady, it is now our time,
That have stood by and seen our wishes prosper,
To cry, good joy: good joy, my lord and lady!

GRA. My Lord Bassanio and my gentle lady,
I wish you all the joy that you can wish;
For I am sure you can wish none from me:
And when your honours mean to solemnize
The bargain of your faith, I do beseech you,
Even at that time I may be married too.

BASS. With all my heart, so thou canst get a wife.

GRA. I thank your lordship, you have got me one.
My eyes, my lord, can look as swift as yours:
You saw the mistress, I beheld the maid;
You loved, I loved for intermission.[6]

---

6. *for intermission*] here, for want of something to do.

No more pertains to me, my lord, than you.
Your fortune stood upon the casket there,
And so did mine too, as the matter falls;
For wooing here until I sweat again,
And swearing till my very roof was dry
With oaths of love, at last, if promise last,
I got a promise of this fair one here
To have her love, provided that your fortune
Achieved her mistress.

POR.   Is this true, Nerissa?

NER.   Madam, it is, so you stand pleased withal.

BASS.   And do you, Gratiano, mean good faith?

GRA.   Yes, faith, my lord.

BASS.   Our feast shall be much honoured in your marriage.

GRA.   We 'll play with them the first boy for a thousand ducats.

NER.   What, and stake down?

GRA.   No; we shall ne'er win at that sport, and stake down.
        But who comes here? Lorenzo and his infidel?
        What, and my old Venetian friend Salerio?

Enter LORENZO, JESSICA, *and* SALERIO, *a Messenger from Venice*

BASS.   Lorenzo and Salerio, welcome hither;
        If that the youth of my new interest here
        Have power to bid you welcome. By your leave,
        I bid my very friends and countrymen,
        Sweet Portia, welcome.

POR.   So do I, my lord:
        They are entirely welcome.

LOR.   I thank your honour. For my part, my lord,
        My purpose was not to have seen you here;
        But meeting with Salerio by the way,
        He did entreat me, past all saying nay,
        To come with him along.

SALER.   I did, my lord;
        And I have reason for it. Signior Antonio
        Commends him to you.   [*Gives* BASSANIO *a letter.*]

BASS.   Ere I ope his letter,
        I pray you, tell me how my good friend doth.

SALER.   Not sick, my lord, unless it be in mind;
      Nor well, unless in mind: his letter there
      Will show you his estate.

GRA.   Nerissa, cheer yon stranger; bid her welcome.
      Your hand, Salerio: what 's the news from Venice?
      How doth that royal merchant,[7] good Antonio?
      I know he will be glad of our success;
      We are the Jasons, we have won the fleece.

SALER.   I would you had won the fleece that he hath lost.

POR.   There are some shrewd contents in yon same paper,
      That steals the colour from Bassanio's cheek:
      Some dear friend dead; else nothing in the world
      Could turn so much the constitution
      Of any constant man. What, worse and worse!
      With leave, Bassanio; I am half yourself,
      And I must freely have the half of anything
      That this same paper brings you.

BASS.   O sweet Portia,
      Here are a few of the unpleasant'st words
      That ever blotted paper! Gentle lady,
      When I did first impart my love to you,
      I freely told you, all the wealth I had
      Ran in my veins, I was a gentleman;
      And then I told you true: and yet, dear lady,
      Rating myself at nothing, you shall see
      How much I was a braggart. When I told you
      My state was nothing, I should then have told you
      That I was worse than nothing; for, indeed,
      I have engaged myself to a dear friend,
      Engaged my friend to his mere enemy,
      To feed my means. Here is a letter, lady;
      The paper as the body of my friend,

---

7. *royal merchant*] This term was specifically allotted to the Venetian merchants who enjoyed a license from the Republic to occupy and govern islands in the Greek Archipelago on the sole condition of acknowledging the suzerainty of the Republic. But it may well be that the epithet "royal" has no more recondite significance than that of "great" or "magnificent."

And every word in it a gaping wound,
Issuing life-blood. But is it true, Salerio?
Have all his ventures fail'd? What, not one hit?
From Tripolis, from Mexico, and England,
From Lisbon, Barbary, and India?
And not one vessel scape the dreadful touch
Of merchant-marring rocks?

SALER.   Not one, my lord.
Besides, it should appear, that if he had
The present money to discharge the Jew,
He would not take it. Never did I know
A creature, that did bear the shape of man,
So keen and greedy to confound a man:
He plies the Duke at morning and at night;
And doth impeach the freedom of the state,
If they deny him justice: twenty merchants,
The Duke himself, and the magnificoes
Of greatest port, have all persuaded with him;
But none can drive him from the envious plea
Of forfeiture, of justice, and his bond.

JES.   When I was with him I have heard him swear
To Tubal and to Chus, his countrymen,
That he would rather have Antonio's flesh
Than twenty times the value of the sum
That he did owe him: and I know, my lord,
If law, authority and power deny not,
It will go hard with poor Antonio.

POR.   Is it your dear friend that is thus in trouble?

BASS.   The dearest friend to me, the kindest man,
The best-condition'd and unwearied spirit
In doing courtesies; and one in whom
The ancient Roman honour more appears
Than any that draws breath in Italy.

POR.   What sum owes he the Jew?

BASS.   For me three thousand ducats.

POR.   What, no more?
Pay him six thousand, and deface the bond;

Double six thousand, and then treble that,
Before a friend of this description
Shall lose a hair through Bassanio's fault.
First go with me to church and call me wife,
And then away to Venice to your friend;
For never shall you lie by Portia's side
With an unquiet soul. You shall have gold
To pay the petty debt twenty times over:
When it is paid, bring your true friend along.
My maid Nerissa and myself meantime
Will live as maids and widows. Come, away!
For you shall hence upon your wedding-day:
Bid your friends welcome, show a merry cheer:
Since you are dear bought, I will love you dear.
But let me hear the letter of your friend.

BASS.   [*Reads*] Sweet Bassanio, my ships have all miscarried, my creditors grow cruel, my estate is very low, my bond to the Jew is forfeit; and since in paying it, it is impossible I should live, all debts are cleared between you and I, if I might but see you at my death. Notwithstanding, use your pleasure: if your love do not persuade you to come, let not my letter.

POR.   O love, dispatch all business, and be gone!
BASS.   Since I have your good leave to go away,
    I will make haste: but, till I come again,
    No bed shall e'er be guilty of my stay,
        No rest be interposer 'twixt us twain.   [*Exeunt.*]

Scene III. *Venice. A street.*

Enter Shylock, Salarino, Antonio, *and* Gaoler

Shy.   Gaoler, look to him: tell not me of mercy;
　　　This is the fool that lent out money gratis:
　　　Gaoler, look to him.
Ant.   Hear me yet, good Shylock.
Shy.   I 'll have my bond; speak not against my bond:
　　　I have sworn an oath that I will have my bond.
　　　Thou call'dst me dog before thou hadst a cause;
　　　But, since I am a dog, beware my fangs:
　　　The Duke shall grant me justice. I do wonder,
　　　Thou naughty gaoler, that thou art so fond
　　　To come abroad with him at his request.
Ant.   I pray thee, hear me speak.
Shy.   I 'll have my bond; I will not hear thee speak:
　　　I 'll have my bond; and therefore speak no more.
　　　I 'll not be made a soft and dull-eyed fool,
　　　To shake the head, relent, and sigh, and yield
　　　To Christian intercessors. Follow not;
　　　I 'll have no speaking: I will have my bond.   [*Exit.*]
Salar.   It is the most impenetrable cur
　　　That ever kept with men.
Ant.   Let him alone:
　　　I 'll follow him no more with bootless prayers.
　　　He seeks my life; his reason well I know:
　　　I oft deliver'd from his forfeitures
　　　Many that have at times made moan to me;
　　　Therefore he hates me.
Salar.   I am sure the Duke
　　　Will never grant this forfeiture to hold.
Ant.   The Duke cannot deny the course of law:
　　　For the commodity that strangers have

With us in Venice, if it be denied,
Will much impeach the justice of his state;
Since that the trade and profit of the city
Consisteth of all nations. Therefore, go:
These griefs and losses have so bated me,
That I shall hardly spare a pound of flesh
To-morrow to my bloody creditor.
Well, gaoler, on. Pray God, Bassanio come
To see me pay his debt, and then I care not!　　　　　*[Exeunt.]*

SCENE IV. *Belmont.* A *room in* PORTIA'S *house.*

Enter PORTIA, NERISSA, LORENZO, JESSICA, *and* BALTHASAR

LOR.　Madam, although I speak it in your presence,
　　　You have a noble and a true conceit
　　　Of god-like amity; which appears most strongly
　　　In bearing thus the absence of your lord.
　　　But if you knew to whom you show this honour,
　　　How true a gentleman you send relief,
　　　How dear a lover of my lord your husband,
　　　I know you would be prouder of the work
　　　Than customary bounty can enforce you.
POR.　I never did repent for doing good,
　　　Nor shall not now: for in companions
　　　That do converse and waste the time together,
　　　Whose souls do bear an equal yoke of love,
　　　There must be needs a like proportion
　　　Of lineaments, of manners and of spirit;
　　　Which makes me think that this Antonio,
　　　Being the bosom lover of my lord,
　　　Must needs be like my lord. If it be so,
　　　How little is the cost I have bestow'd
　　　In purchasing the semblance of my soul

From out the state of hellish misery!
This comes too near the praising of myself;
Therefore no more of it: hear other things.
Lorenzo, I commit into your hands
The husbandry and manage of my house
Until my lord's return: for mine own part,
I have toward heaven breathed a secret VOW
To live in prayer and contemplation,
Only attended by Nerissa here,
Until her husband and my lord's return:
There is a monastery two miles off;
And there will we abide. I do desire you
Not to deny this imposition;
The which my love and some necessity
Now lays upon you.
LOR.   Madam, with all my heart;
I shall obey you in all fair commands.
POR.   My people do already know my mind,
And will acknowledge you and Jessica
In place of Lord Bassanio and myself.
And so farewell, till we shall meet again.
LOR.   Fair thoughts and happy hours attend on you!
JES.   I wish your ladyship all heart's content.
POR.   I thank you for your wish, and am well pleased
To wish it back on you: fare you well, Jessica.
                              [*Exeunt* JESSICA *and* LORENZO.]
Now, Balthasar,
As I have ever found thee honest-true,
So let me find thee still. Take this same letter,
And use thou all the endeavour of a man
In speed to Padua: see thou render this
Into my cousin's hand, Doctor Bellario;
And, look, what notes and garments he doth give thee,
Bring them, I pray thee, with imagined speed
Unto the tranect,[1] to the common ferry

---

1. *tranect*] a word possibly corrupted from the Italian *traghetto* (ferry).

Which trades to Venice. Waste no time in words,
But get thee gone: I shall be there before thee.

BALTH.   Madam, I go with all convenient speed.   [*Exit.*]

POR.   Come on, Nerissa; I have work in hand
That you yet know not of; we'll see our husbands
Before they think of us.

NER.   Shall they see us?

POR.   They shall, Nerissa; but in such a habit,
That they shall think we are accomplished
With that we lack. I 'll hold thee any wager,
When we are both accoutred like young men,
I 'll prove the prettier fellow of the two,
And wear my dagger with the braver grace,
And speak between the change of man and boy
With a reed voice, and turn two mincing steps
Into a manly stride, and speak of frays
Like a fine bragging youth; and tell quaint lies
How honourable ladies sought my love,
Which I denying, they fell sick and died;
I could not do withal:[2] then I 'll repent,
And wish, for all that, that I had not kill'd them;
And twenty of these puny lies I 'll tell,
That men shall swear I have discontinued school
Above a twelvemonth. I have within my mind
A thousand raw tricks of these bragging Jacks,
Which I will practise.

NER.   Why, shall we turn to men?

POR.   Fie, what a question 's that,
If thou wert near a lewd interpreter!
But come, I 'll tell thee all my whole device
When I am in my coach, which stays for us
At the park-gate; and therefore haste away,
For we must measure twenty miles to-day.   [*Exeunt.*]

---

2. *I could not do withal*] I could not help it; a common phrase in contemporary authors.

SCENE V. *The same. A garden.*

Enter LAUNCELOT *and* JESSICA

LAUN.   Yes, truly; for, look you, the sins of the father are to be laid upon the children: therefore, I promise ye, I fear you.[1] I was always plain with you, and so now I speak my agitation[2] of the matter; therefore be of good cheer; for, truly, I think you are damned. There is but one hope in it that can do you any good; and that is but a kind of bastard hope neither.

JES.   And what hope is that, I pray thee?

LAUN.   Marry, you may partly hope that your father got you not, that you are not the Jew's daughter.

JES.   That were a kind of bastard hope, indeed: so the sins of my mother should be visited upon me.

LAUN.   Truly then I fear you are damned both by father and mother: thus when I shun Scylla, your father, I fall into Charybdis, your mother:[3] well, you are gone both ways.

JES.   I shall be saved by my husband; he hath made me a Christian.

LAUN.   Truly, the more to blame he: we were Christians enow before; e'en as many as could well live, one by another. This making of Christians will raise the price of hogs: if we grow all to be pork-eaters, we shall not shortly have a rasher on the coals for money.

Enter LORENZO

JES.   I 'll tell my husband, Launcelot, what you say: here he comes.

---

1. *I fear you*] I fear for you.
2. *agitation*] A clownish blunder for "cogitation."
3. *Scylla . . . Charybdis*] This proverb, which is very common in Elizabethan authors, seems to have been the invention of a twelfth-century Latin poet, Philippe Gualtier de Chatillon, whose Latin epic *Alexandreis* includes the line: "Incidis in Scyllam, cupiens vitare Charybdim" ("You encounter Scylla when attempting to avoid Charybdis").

LOR.   I shall grow jealous of you shortly, Launcelot, if you thus get my wife into corners.

JES.   Nay, you need not fear us, Lorenzo: Launcelot and I are out. He tells me flatly, there is no mercy for me in heaven, because I am a Jew's daughter: and he says, you are no good member of the commonwealth; for, in converting Jews to Christians, you raise the price of pork.

LOR.   I shall answer that better to the commonwealth than you can the getting up of the negro's belly: the Moor is with child by you, Launcelot.

LAUN.   It is much that the Moor should be more than reason: but if she be less than an honest woman, she is indeed more than I took her for.

LOR.   How every fool can play upon the word! I think the best grace of wit will shortly turn into silence; and discourse grow commendable in none only but parrots. Go in, sirrah; bid them prepare for dinner.

LAUN.   That is done, sir; they have all stomachs.

LOR.   Goodly Lord, what a wit-snapper are you! then bid them prepare dinner.

LAUN.   That is done too, sir; only "cover" is the word.

LOR.   Will you cover,[4] then, sir?

LAUN.   Not so, sir, neither; I know my duty.

LOR.   Yet more quarrelling with occasion! Wilt thou show the whole wealth of thy wit in an instant? I pray thee, understand a plain man in his plain meaning: go to thy fellows; bid them cover the table, serve in the meat, and we will come in to dinner.

LAUN.   For the table, sir, it shall be served in; for the meat, sir, it shall be covered; for your coming in to dinner, sir, why, let it be as humours and conceits shall govern.   [*Exit.*]

LOR.   O dear discretion, how his words are suited!
       The fool hath planted in his memory
       An army of good words; and I do know
       A many fools, that stand in better place,
       Garnish'd like him, that for a tricksy word

---

4. *cover*] The clown quibbles on the use of the word "cover" in the two senses of laying the table and wearing one's hat.

Defy the matter. How cheer'st thou, Jessica?
And now, good sweet, say thy opinion,
How dost thou like the Lord Bassanio's wife?

JES.   Past all expressing. It is very meet
The Lord Bassanio live an upright life;
For, having such a blessing in his lady,
He finds the joys of heaven here on earth;
And if on earth he do not mean it, then
In reason he should never come to heaven.
Why, if two gods should play some heavenly match
And on the wager lay two earthly women,
And Portia one, there must be something else
Pawn'd with the other; for the poor rude world
Hath not her fellow.

LOR.   Even such a husband
Hast thou of me as she is for a wife.

JES.   Nay, but ask my opinion too of that.

LOR.   I will anon: first, let us go to dinner.

JES.   Nay, let me praise you while I have a stomach.

LOR.   No, pray thee, let it serve for table-talk;
Then, howsoe'er thou speak'st, 'mong other things
I shall digest it.

JES.   Well, I 'll set you forth.   [*Exeunt.*]

ACT IV.

SCENE I. *Venice. A Court of Justice.*

Enter the DUKE, *the* Magnificoes, ANTONIO, BASSANIO, GRATIANO, SALERIO, *and others*

DUKE.   What, is Antonio here?

ANT.   Ready, so please your Grace.

DUKE.   I am sorry for thee: thou art come to answer
    A stony adversary, an inhuman wretch
    Uncapable of pity, void and empty
    From any dram of mercy.

ANT.   I have heard
    Your Grace hath ta'en great pains to qualify
    His rigorous course; but since he stands obdurate,
    And that no lawful means can carry me
    Out of his envy's reach, I do oppose
    My patience to his fury; and am arm'd
    To suffer, with a quietness of spirit,
    The very tyranny and rage of his.

DUKE.   Go one, and call the Jew into the court.

SALER.   He is ready at the door: he comes, my lord.

Enter SHYLOCK

DUKE.   Make room, and let him stand before our face.
    Shylock, the world thinks, and I think so too,
    That thou but lead'st this fashion of thy malice
    To the last hour of act; and then 't is thought
    Thou 'lt show thy mercy and remorse more strange

Than is thy strange apparent cruelty;
And where thou now exact'st the penalty,
Which is a pound of this poor merchant's flesh,
Thou wilt not only loose the forfeiture,
But, touch'd with human gentleness and love,
Forgive a moiety of the principal;
Glancing an eye of pity on his losses,
That have of late so huddled on his back,
Enow to press a royal merchant down,
And pluck commiseration of his state
From brassy bosoms and rough hearts of flint,
From stubborn Turks and Tartars, never train'd
To offices of tender courtesy.
We all expect a gentle answer, Jew.

SHY. I have possess'd your Grace of what I purpose;
And by our holy Sabbath have I sworn
To have the due and forfeit of my bond:
If you deny it, let the danger light
Upon your charter and your city's freedom.
You 'll ask me, why I rather choose to have
A weight of carrion-flesh than to receive
Three thousand ducats: I 'll not answer that:
But, say, it is my humour: is it answer'd?
What if my house be troubled with a rat,
And I be pleased to give ten thousand ducats
To have it baned? What, are you answer'd yet?
Some men there are love not a gaping pig;[1]
Some, that are mad if they behold a cat;
And others, when the bagpipe sings i' the nose,
Cannot contain their urine: for affection,
Mistress of passion, sways it to the mood
Of what it likes or loathes. Now, for your answer:
As there is no firm reason to be render'd,
Why he cannot abide a gaping pig;
Why he, a harmless necessary cat;

---

1. *gaping pig*] a pig prepared for the table with a lemon in its mouth.

Why he, a woollen bag-pipe; but of force
Must yield to such inevitable shame
As to offend, himself being offended;
So can I give no reason, nor I will not,
More than a lodged hate and a certain loathing
I bear Antonio, that I follow thus
A losing suit against him. Are you answer'd?

BASS.   This is no answer, thou unfeeling man,
To excuse the current of thy cruelty.

SHY.   I am not bound to please thee with my answer.

BASS.   Do all men kill the things they do not love?

SHY.   Hates any man the thing he would not kill?

BASS.   Every offence is not a hate at first.

SHY.   What, wouldst thou have a serpent sting thee twice?

ANT.   I pray you, think you question with the Jew:[2]
You may as well go stand upon the beach,
And bid the main flood bate his usual height;
You may as well use question with the wolf,
Why he hath made the ewe bleat for the lamb;
You may as well forbid the mountain pines
To wag their high tops, and to make no noise,
When they are fretten with the gusts of heaven;
You may as well do any thing most hard,
As seek to soften that — than which what's harder? —
His Jewish heart: therefore, I do beseech you,
Make no more offers, use no farther means,
But with all brief and plain conveniency
Let me have judgement and the Jew his will.

BASS.   For thy three thousand ducats here is six.

SHY.   If every ducat in six thousand ducats
Were in six parts and every part a ducat,
I would not draw them; I would have my bond.

DUKE.   How shalt thou hope for mercy, rendering none?

SHY.   What judgement shall I dread, doing no wrong?

---

2. *think you . . . Jew*] remember you are conversing with, seeking to move the inflexible Jew.

You have among you many a purchased slave,
Which, like your asses and your dogs and mules,
You use in abject and in slavish parts,
Because you bought them: shall I say to you,
Let them be free, marry them to your heirs?
Why sweat they under burthens? let their beds
Be made as soft as yours, and let their palates
Be season'd with such viands? You will answer
"The slaves are ours:" so do I answer you:
The pound of flesh, which I demand of him,
Is dearly bought; 't is mine and I will have it.
If you deny me, fie upon your law!
There is no force in the decrees of Venice.
I stand for judgement: answer; shall I have it?

DUKE. Upon my power I may dismiss this court,
Unless Bellario, a learned doctor,
Whom I have sent for to determine this,
Come here to-day.

SALER.   My lord, here stays without
A messenger with letters from the doctor,
New come from Padua.

DUKE. Bring us the letters; call the messenger.

BASS. Good cheer, Antonio! What, man, courage yet!
The Jew shall have my flesh, blood, bones, and all,
Ere thou shalt lose for me one drop of blood.

ANT. I am a tainted wether[3] of the flock,
Meetest for death: the weakest kind of fruit
Drops earliest to the ground; and so let me:
You cannot better be employ'd, Bassanio,
Than to live still, and write mine epitaph.

Enter NERISSA, *dressed like a lawyer's clerk*

DUKE. Came you from Padua, from Bellario?

NER. From both, my lord. Bellario greets your Grace.

                              [*Presenting a letter.*]

---

3. *wether*] castrated ram.

BASS. Why dost thou whet thy knife so earnestly?
SHY. To cut the forfeiture from that bankrupt there.
GRA. Not on thy sole, but on thy soul, harsh Jew,
  Thou makest thy knife keen; but no metal can,
  No, not the hangman's axe, bear half the keenness
  Of thy sharp envy. Can no prayers pierce thee?
SHY. No, none that thou hast wit enough to make.
GRA. O, be thou damn'd, inexecrable dog!
  And for thy life let justice be accused.
  Thou almost makest me waver in my faith,
  To hold opinion with Pythagoras,
  That souls of animals infuse themselves
  Into the trunks of men: thy currish spirit
  Govern'd a wolf, who hang'd for human slaughter,
  Even from the gallows did his fell soul fleet,
  And, whilst thou lay'st in thy unhallow'd dam,
  Infused itself in thee; for thy desires
  Are wolvish, bloody, starved and ravenous.
SHY. Till thou canst rail the seal from off my bond,
  Thou but offend'st thy lungs to speak so loud:
  Repair thy wit, good youth, or it will fall
  To cureless ruin. I stand here for law.
DUKE. This letter from Bellario doth commend
  A young and learned doctor to our court.
  Where is he?
NER.   He attendeth here hard by,
  To know your answer, whether you 'll admit him.
DUKE. With all my heart. Some three or four of you
  Go give him courteous conduct to this place.
  Meantime the court shall hear Bellario's letter.
CLERK. [Reads] Your Grace shall understand that at the receipt of your letter
  I am very sick: but in the instant that your messenger came, in loving
  visitation was with me a young doctor of Rome; his name is Balthasar. I
  acquainted him with the cause in controversy between the Jew and
  Antonio the merchant: we turned o'er many books together: he is
  furnished with my opinion; which, bettered with his own learning, —
  the greatness whereof I cannot enough commend, — comes with him,
  at my importunity, to fill up your Grace's request in my stead. I beseech
  you, let his lack of years be no impediment to let him lack a reverend

estimation; for I never knew so young a body with so old a head. I leave him to your gracious acceptance, whose trial shall better publish his commendation.

DUKE.   You hear the learn'd Bellario, what he writes:
And here, I take it, is the doctor come.

Enter PORTIA *for* BALTHASAR

Give me your hand. Come you from old Bellario?
POR.   I did, my lord.
DUKE.   You are welcome: take your place.
Are you acquainted with the difference
That holds this present question in the court?
POR.   I am informed throughly of the cause.
Which is the merchant here, and which the Jew?
DUKE.   Antonio and old Shylock, both stand forth.
POR.   Is your name Shylock?
SHY.   Shylock is my name.
POR.   Of a strange nature is the suit you follow;
Yet in such rule that the Venetian law
Cannot impugn you as you do proceed.
You stand within his danger,[4] do you not?
ANT.   Ay, so he says.
POR.   Do you confess the bond?
ANT.   I do.
POR.   Then must the Jew be merciful.
SHY.   On what compulsion must I? tell me that.
POR.   The quality of mercy is not strain'd,[5]
It droppeth as the gentle rain from heaven
Upon the place beneath: it is twice blest;
It blesseth him that gives, and him that takes:

---

4. *within his danger*] in his power. The original meaning of danger was not, as in modern times, "peril," but "dominion," including the power to hurt or harm.
5. *strain'd*] compelled, moved by force or compulsion. Portia takes up the challenge conveyed in Shylock's query, "On what compulsion must I?"

'T is mightiest in the mightiest: it becomes
The throned monarch better than his crown;
His sceptre shows the force of temporal power,
The attribute to awe and majesty,
Wherein doth sit the dread and fear of kings;
But mercy is above this sceptred sway;
It is enthroned in the hearts of kings,
It is an attribute to God himself;
And earthly power doth then show likest God's
When mercy seasons justice. Therefore, Jew,
Though justice be thy plea, consider this,
That, in the course of justice, none of us
Should see salvation: we do pray for mercy;
And that same prayer doth teach us all to render
The deeds of mercy. I have spoke thus much
To mitigate the justice of thy plea;
Which if thou follow, this strict court of Venice
Must needs give sentence 'gainst the merchant there.

SHY.   My deeds upon my head! I crave the law,
The penalty and forfeit of my bond.

POR.   Is he not able to discharge the money?

BASS.   Yes, here I tender it for him in the court;
Yea, twice the sum: if that will not suffice,
I will be bound to pay it ten times o'er,
On forfeit of my hands, my head, my heart:
If this will not suffice, it must appear
That malice bears down truth. And I beseech you,
Wrest once the law to your authority:
To do a great right, do a little wrong,
And curb this cruel devil of his will.

POR.   It must not be; there is no power in Venice
Can alter a decree established:
'T will be recorded for a precedent,
And many an error, by the same example,
Will rush into the state: it cannot be.

SHY.   A Daniel come to judgement! yea, a Daniel!

O wise young judge,[6] how I do honour thee!

POR.   I pray you, let me look upon the bond.

SHY.   Here 't is, most reverend doctor, here it is.

POR.   Shylock, there 's thrice thy money offer'd thee.

SHY.   An oath, an oath, I have an oath in heaven:
Shall I lay perjury upon my soul?
No, not for Venice.

POR.   Why, this bond is forfeit;
And lawfully by this the Jew may claim
A pound of flesh, to be by him cut off
Nearest the merchant's heart. Be merciful:
Take thrice thy money; bid me tear the bond.

SHY.   When it is paid according to the tenour.
It doth appear you are a worthy judge;
You know the law, your exposition
Hath been most sound: I charge you by the law,
Whereof you are a well-deserving pillar,
Proceed to judgement: by my soul I swear
There is no power in the tongue of man
To alter me: I stay here on my bond.

ANT.   Most heartily I do beseech the court
To give the judgement.

POR.   Why then, thus it is:
You must prepare your bosom for his knife.

SHY.   O noble judge! O excellent young man!

POR.   For the intent and purpose of the law
Hath full relation to the penalty,
Which here appeareth due upon the bond.

SHY.   'T is very true: O wise and upright judge!
How much more elder art thou than thy looks!

POR.   Therefore lay bare your bosom.

SHY.   Ay, his breast:
So says the bond: — doth it not, noble judge? —

---

6. A *Daniel . . . young judge*] The allusion is to the "History of Susannah" in the *Apocrypha*, where Daniel, "a young youth" (v. 45) convicted the elders "of false witness by their own mouth" (v. 61), and "from that day forth was had in great reputation in the sight of the people" (v. 64).

"Nearest his heart:" those are the very words.

POR.   It is so. Are there balance[7] here to weigh
        The flesh?

SHY.   I have them ready.

POR.   Have by some surgeon, Shylock, on your charge,
        To stop his wounds, lest he do bleed to death.

SHY.   Is it so nominated in the bond?

POR.   It is not so express'd: but what of that?
        'T were good you do so much for charity.

SHY.   I cannot find it; 't is not in the bond.

POR.   You, merchant, have you any thing to say?

ANT.   But little: I am arm'd and well prepared.
        Give me your hand, Bassanio: fare you well!
        Grieve not that I am fallen to this for you;
        For herein Fortune shows herself more kind
        Than is her custom: it is still her use
        To let the wretched man outlive his wealth,
        To view with hollow eye and wrinkled brow
        An age of poverty; from which lingering penance
        Of such misery doth she cut me off.
        Commend me to your honourable wife:
        Tell her the process of Antonio's end;
        Say how I loved you, speak me fair in death;
        And, when the tale is told, bid her be judge
        Whether Bassanio had not once a love.
        Repent but you that you shall lose your friend,
        And he repents not that he pays your debt;
        For if the Jew do cut but deep enough,
        I 'll pay it presently with all my heart.

BASS. Antonio, I am married to a wife
        Which is as dear to me as life itself;
        But life itself, my wife, and all the world,
        Are not with me esteem'd above thy life:
        I would lose all, ay, sacrifice them all
        Here to this devil, to deliver you.

---

7. *balance*] commonly treated as a plural noun with the sense of "scales."

POR.   Your wife would give you little thanks for that,
    If she were by, to hear you make the offer.
GRA.   I have a wife, whom, I protest, I love:
    I would she were in heaven, so she could
    Entreat some power to change this currish Jew.
NER.   'T is well you offer it behind her back;
    The wish would make else an unquiet house.
SHY.   These be the Christian husbands. I have a daughter;
    Would any of the stock of Barrabas[8]
    Had been her husband rather than a Christian!   *[Aside.]*
    We trifle time: I pray thee, pursue sentence.
POR.   A pound of that same merchant's flesh is thine:
    The court awards it, and the law doth give it.
SHY.   Most rightful judge!
POR.   And you must cut this flesh from off his breast:
    The law allows it, and the court awards it.
SHY.   Most learned judge! A sentence! Come, prepare!
POR.   Tarry a little; there is something else.
    This bond doth give thee here no jot of blood;
    The words expressly are "a pound of flesh:"
    Take then thy bond, take thou thy pound of flesh:
    But, in the cutting it, if thou dost shed
    One drop of Christian blood, thy lands and goods
    Are, by the laws of Venice, confiscate
    Unto the state of Venice.
GRA.   O upright judge! Mark, Jew: O learned judge!
SHY.   Is that the law?
POR.   Thyself shalt see the act:
    For, as thou urgest justice, be assured
    Thou shalt have justice, more than thou desirest.
GRA.   O learned judge! Mark, Jew: a learned judge!
SHY.   I take this offer, then; pay the bond thrice,
    And let the Christian go.
BASS.   Here is the money.

---

8. *Barrabas*] In New Testament accounts, when Pilate allowed the people of Jerusalem to
choose a prisoner to be released in honor of the Passover they chose Barrabas rather than
Jesus.

POR.   Soft!
    The Jew shall have all justice; soft! no haste:
    He shall have nothing but the penalty.
GRA.   O Jew! an upright judge, a learned judge!
POR.   Therefore prepare thee to cut off the flesh.
    Shed thou no blood; nor cut thou less nor more
    But just a pound of flesh: if thou cut'st more
    Or less than a just pound, be it but so much
    As makes it light or heavy in the substance,
    Or the division of the twentieth part
    Of one poor scruple, nay, if the scale do turn
    But in the estimation of a hair,
    Thou diest and all thy goods are confiscate.
GRA.   A second Daniel, a Daniel, Jew!
    Now, infidel, I have you on the hip.
POR.   Why doth the Jew pause? take thy forfeiture.
SHY.   Give me my principal, and let me go.
BASS.   I have it ready for thee; here it is.
POR.   He hath refused it in the open court:
    He shall have merely justice and his bond.
GRA.   A Daniel, still say I, a second Daniel!
    I thank thee, Jew, for teaching me that word.
SHY.   Shall I not have barely my principal?
POR.   Thou shalt have nothing but the forfeiture,
    To be so taken at thy peril, Jew.
SHY.   Why, then the devil give him good of it!
    I 'll stay no longer question.
POR.   Tarry, Jew:
    The law hath yet another hold on you.
    It is enacted in the laws of Venice,
    If it be proved against an alien
    That by direct or indirect attempts
    He seek the life of any citizen,
    The party 'gainst the which he doth contrive
    Shall seize one half his goods; the other half
    Comes to the privy coffer of the state;
    And the offender's life lies in the mercy

Of the Duke only, 'gainst all other voice.
In which predicament, I say, thou stand'st;
For it appears, by manifest proceeding,
That indirectly, and directly too,
Thou hast contrived against the very life
Of the defendant; and thou hast incurr'd
The danger formerly by me rehearsed.
Down, therefore, and beg mercy of the Duke.

GRA.   Beg that thou mayst have leave to hang thyself:
And yet, thy wealth being forfeit to the state,
Thou hast not left the value of a cord;
Therefore thou must be hang'd at the state's charge.

DUKE.   That thou shall see the difference of our spirits,
I pardon thee thy life before thou ask it:
For half thy wealth, it is Antonio's;
The other half comes to the general state,
Which humbleness may drive unto a fine.

POR.   Ay, for the state, not for Antonio.

SHY.   Nay, take my life and all; pardon not that:
You take my house, when you do take the prop
That doth sustain my house; you take my life,
When you do take the means whereby I live.

POR.   What mercy can you render him, Antonio?

GRA.   A halter gratis; nothing else, for God's sake.

ANT.   So please my lord the Duke and all the court
To quit the fine for one half of his goods,
I am content; so he will let me have
The other half in use,[9] to render it,
Upon his death, unto the gentleman
That lately stole his daughter:
Two things provided more, that, for this favour,
He presently become a Christian;
The other, that he do record a gift,
Here in the court, of all he dies possess'd,
Unto his son Lorenzo and his daughter.

---

9. *in use*] in trust.

DUKE.   He shall do this, or else I do recant
    The pardon that I late pronounced here.
POR.   Art thou contented, Jew? what dost thou say?
SHY.   I am content.
POR.   Clerk, draw a deed of gift.
SHY.   I pray you, give me leave to go from hence;
    I am not well: send the deed after me,
    And I will sign it.
DUKE.   Get thee gone, but do it.
GRA.   In christening shalt thou have two godfathers:
    Had I been judge, thou shouldst have had ten more,[10]
    To bring thee to the gallows, not the font.   [*Exit* SHYLOCK.]
DUKE.   Sir, I entreat you home with me to dinner.
POR.   I humbly do desire your Grace of pardon:
    I must away this night toward Padua,
    And it is meet I presently set forth.
DUKE.   I am sorry that your leisure serves you not.
    Antonio, gratify this gentleman,
    For, in my mind, you are much bound to him.
                     [*Exeunt* DUKE *and his train.*]
BASS.   Most worthy gentleman, I and my friend
    Have by your wisdom been this day acquitted
    Of grievous penalties; in lieu whereof,
    Three thousand ducats, due unto the Jew,
    We freely cope[11] your courteous pains withal.
ANT.   And stand indebted, over and above,
    In love and service to you evermore.
POR.   He is well paid that is well satisfied;
    And I, delivering you, am satisfied,
    And therein do account myself well paid:
    My mind was never yet more mercenary.
    I pray you, know me when we meet again:
    I wish you well, and so I take my leave.

---

10. *ten more*] a jury of twelve men.
11. *cope*] requite, give the equivalent of.

BASS.   Dear sir, of force I must attempt you further:
    Take some remembrance of us, as a tribute,
    Not as a fee: grant me two things, I pray you,
    Not to deny me, and to pardon me.
POR.   You press me far, and therefore I will yield.
    Give me your gloves, I 'll wear them for your sake; [*To* ANTONIO.]
    And, for your love I 'll take this ring from you: [*To* BASSANIO.]
    Do not draw back your hand; I 'll take no more;
    And you in love shall not deny me this.
BASS.   This ring, good sir, alas, it is a trifle!
    I will not shame myself to give you this.
POR.   I will have nothing else but only this;
    And now methinks I have a mind to it.
BASS.   There 's more depends on this than on the value.
    The dearest ring in Venice will I give you,
    And find it out by proclamation:
    Only for this, I pray you, pardon me.
POR.   I see, sir, you are liberal in offers:
    You taught me first to beg; and now methinks
    You teach me how a beggar should be answer'd.
BASS.   Good sir, this ring was given me by my wife;
    And when she put it on, she made me vow
    That I should neither sell nor give nor lose it.
POR.   That 'scuse serves many men to save their gifts.
    An if your wife be not a mad-woman,
    And know how well I have deserved the ring,
    She would not hold out enemy for ever,
    For giving it to me. Well, peace be with you!
                     [*Exeunt* PORTIA *and* NERISSA.]
ANT.   My Lord Bassanio, let him have the ring:
    Let his deservings and my love withal
    Be valued 'gainst your wife's commandment.
BASS.   Go, Gratiano, run and overtake him;
    Give him the ring; and bring him, if thou canst,
    Unto Antonio's house: away! make haste.   [*Exit* GRATIANO.]
    Come, you and I will thither presently;
    And in the morning early will we both
    Fly toward Belmont: come, Antonio.   [*Exeunt.*]

SCENE II. *The same. A street.*

Enter PORTIA *and* NERISSA

POR.   Inquire the Jew's house out, give him this deed
        And let him sign it: we 'll away to-night
        And be a day before our husbands home:
        This deed will be well welcome to Lorenzo.

Enter GRATIANO

GRA.   Fair sir, you are well o'erta'en:
        My Lord Bassanio upon more advice
        Hath sent you here this ring, and doth entreat
        Your company at dinner.
POR.   That cannot be:
        His ring I do accept most thankfully:
        And so, I pray you, tell him: furthermore,
        I pray you, show my youth old Shylock's house.
GRA.   That will I do.
NER.   Sir, I would speak with you.
        I 'll see if I can get my husband's ring,   [*Aside to* PORTIA.]
        Which I did make him swear to keep for ever.
POR.   [*Aside to* NERISSA.] Thou mayst, I warrant. We shall have old[1]
        swearing
        That they did give the rings away to men;
        But we 'll outface them, and outswear them too.
        [*Aloud*] Away! make haste: thou know'st where I will tarry!
NER.   Come, good sir, will you show me to this house?
                                                        [*Exeunt.*]

---

1. *old*] any amount of.

ACT V.

SCENE I. *Belmont. Avenue to* PORTIA'S *house.*

Enter LORENZO *and* JESSICA

LOR.   The moon shines bright: in such a night as this,
       When the sweet wind did gently kiss the trees
       And they did make no noise, in such a night
       Troilus methinks mounted the Troyan walls,
       And sighed his soul toward the Grecian tents,
       Where Cressid lay that night.
JES.   In such a night
       Did Thisbe fearfully o'ertrip the dew,
       And saw the lion's shadow ere himself,
       And ran dismay'd away.
LOR.   In such a night
       Stood Dido with a willow in her hand
       Upon the wild sea banks, and waft her love
       To come again to Carthage.
JES.   In such a night
       Medea gather'd the enchanted herbs
       That did renew old Æson.[1]
LOR.   In such a night
       Did Jessica steal from the wealthy Jew,

---

1. *Troilus . . . Æson*]. The allusions to Troilus and Cressid probably refer to Chaucer's
Troylus and Cresseide; Thisbe is Chaucer's second subject in his *Legend of Good Women*
and the tale of Dido is the third, followed by the legend of Medea and Æson (Jason).

And with an unthrift love did run from Venice
As far as Belmont.

JES.   In such a night
Did young Lorenzo swear he loved her well,
Stealing her soul with many vows of faith
And ne'er a true one.

LOR.   In such a night
Did pretty Jessica, like a little shrew,
Slander her love, and he forgave it her.

JES.   I would out-night you, did no body come;
But, hark, I hear the footing of a man.

Enter STEPHANO

LOR.   Who comes so fast in silence of the night?
STEPH.   A friend.
LOR.   A friend! what friend? your name, I pray you, friend?
STEPH.   Stephano is my name; and I bring word
My mistress will before the break of day
Be here at Belmont: she doth stray about
By holy crosses, where she kneels and prays
For happy wedlock hours.

LOR.   Who comes with her?
STEPH.   None but a holy hermit and her maid.
I pray you, is my master yet return'd?
LOR.   He is not, nor we have not heard from him.
But go we in, I pray thee, Jessica,
And ceremoniously let us prepare
Some welcome for the mistress of the house.

Enter LAUNCELOT

LAUN.   Sola, sola! wo ha, ho! sola, sola!
LOR.   Who calls?
LAUN.   Sola! did you see Master Lorenzo? Master Lorenzo, sola, sola!
LOR.   Leave hollaing, man: here.
LAUN.   Sola! where? where?
LOR.   Here.

LAUN.   Tell him there 's a post come from my master, with his horn full
    of good news: my master will be here ere morning.   [*Exit.*]
LOR.   Sweet soul, let 's in, and there expect their coming.
    And yet no matter: why should we go in?
    My friend Stephano, signify, I pray you,
    Within the house, your mistress is at hand;
    And bring your music forth into the air.   [*Exit* STEPHANO.]
    How sweet the moonlight sleeps upon this bank!
    Here will we sit, and let the sounds of music
    Creep in our ears: soft stillness and the night
    Become the touches of sweet harmony.
    Sit, Jessica. Look how the floor of heaven
    Is thick inlaid with patines of bright gold:
    There 's not the smallest orb which thou behold'st
    But in his motion like an angel sings,
    Still quiring² to the young-eyed cherubins;
    Such harmony is in immortal souls;
    But whilst this muddy vesture of decay
    Doth grossly close it in, we cannot hear it.

Enter Musicians

    Come, ho, and wake Diana with a hymn!
    With sweetest touches pierce your mistress' ear,
    And draw her home with music.   [*Music.*]
JES.   I am never merry when I hear sweet music.
LOR.   The reason is, your spirits are attentive:
    For do but note a wild and wanton herd,
    Or race of youthful and unhandled colts,
    Fetching mad bounds, bellowing and neighing loud,
    Which is the hot condition of their blood;
    If they but hear perchance a trumpet sound,
    Or any air of music touch their ears,
    You shall perceive them make a mutual stand,
    Their savage eyes turn'd to a modest gaze
    By the sweet power of music: therefore the poet

---

2. *quiring*] singing in concert.

Did feign that Orpheus drew trees, stones and floods;
Since nought so stockish, hard and full of rage,
But music for the time doth change his nature.
The man that hath no music in himself,
Nor is not moved with concord of sweet sounds,
Is fit for treasons, stratagems and spoils;
The motions of his spirit are dull as night,
And his affections dark as Erebus:[3]
Let no such man be trusted. Mark the music.

Enter PORTIA *and* NERISSA

POR.   That light we see is burning in my hall.
How far that little candle throws his beams!
So shines a good deed in a naughty world.
NER.   When the moon shone, we did not see the candle.
POR.   So doth the greater glory dim the less:
A substitute shines brightly as a king,
Until a king be by; and then his state
Empties itself, as doth an inland brook
Into the main of waters. Music! hark!
NER.   It is your music, madam, of the house.
POR.   Nothing is good, I see, without respect:[4]
Methinks it sounds much sweeter than by day.
NER.   Silence bestows that virtue on it, madam.
POR.   The crow doth sing as sweetly as the lark,
When neither is attended; and I think
The nightingale, if she should sing by day,
When every goose is cackling, would be thought
No better a musician than the wren.
How many things by season season'd are
To their right praise and true perfection!
Peace, ho! the moon sleeps with Endymion,[5]
And would not be awaked.   [*Music ceases.*]

---

3. *Erebus*] Tartarus, hell.
4. *without respect*] without consideration of circumstances.
5. *Endymion*] a youth loved by the goddess of the moon.

LOR.   That is the voice,
    Or I am much deceived, of Portia.
POR.   He knows me as the blind man knows the cuckoo,
    By the bad voice.
LOR.   Dear lady, welcome home.
POR.   We have been praying for our husbands' healths,
    Which speed, we hope, the better for our words.
    Are they return'd?
LOR.   Madam, they are not yet;
    But there is come a messenger before,
    To signify their coming.
POR.   Go in, Nerissa;
    Give order to my servants that they take
    No note at all of our being absent hence;
    Nor you, Lorenzo; Jessica, nor you.   [A tucket sounds.]
LOR.   Your husband is at hand; I hear his trumpet:
    We are no tell-tales, madam; fear you not.
POR.   This night methinks is but the daylight sick;
    It looks a little paler: 't is a day,
    Such as the day is when the sun is hid.

Enter BASSANIO, ANTONIO, GRATIANO, *and their followers*

BASS.   We should hold day with the Antipodes,[6]
    If you would walk in absence of the sun.
POR.   Let me give light, but let me not be light;
    For a light wife doth make a heavy husband,
    And never be Bassanio so for me:
    But God sort all! You are welcome home, my lord.
BASS.   I thank you, madam. Give welcome to my friend.
    This is the man, this is Antonio,
    To whom I am so infinitely bound.
POR.   You should in all sense be much bound to him,
    For, as I hear, he was much bound for you.
ANT.   No more than I am well acquitted of.
POR.   Sir, you are very welcome to our house:

---

6. *the Antipodes*] the people living on the opposite side of the globe.

It must appear in other ways than words,
Therefore I scant this breathing courtesy.

GRA.   [*To* NERISSA] By yonder moon I swear you do me wrong;
In faith, I gave it to the judge's clerk:
Would he were gelt[7] that had it, for my part,
Since you do take it, love, so much at heart.

POR.   A quarrel, ho, already! what 's the matter?

GRA.   About a hoop of gold, a paltry ring
That she did give me, whose posy[8] was
For all the world like cutler's poetry
Upon a knife, "Love me, and leave me not."

NER.   What talk you of the posy or the value?
You swore to me, when I did give it you,
That you would wear it till your hour of death,
And that it should lie with you in your grave:
Though not for me, yet for your vehement oaths,
You should have been respective, and have kept it.
Gave it a judge's clerk! no, God's my judge,
The clerk will ne'er wear hair on 's face that had it.

GRA.   He will, an if he live to be a man.

NER.   Ay, if a woman live to be a man.

GRA.   Now, by this hand, I gave it to a youth,
A kind of boy, a little scrubbed[9] boy,
No higher than thyself, the judge's clerk,
A prating boy, that begg'd it as a fee:
I could not for my heart deny it him.

POR.   You were to blame, I must be plain with you,
To part so slightly with your wife's first gift;
A thing stuck on with oaths upon your finger
And so riveted with faith unto your flesh.
I gave my love a ring, and made him swear
Never to part with it; and here he stands;

7. *gelt*] castrated.
8. *posy*] inscription on a ring.
9. *scrubbed*] a contemptuous epithet implying both repulsiveness and insignificance.

     I dare be sworn for him he would not leave it
     Nor pluck it from his finger, for the wealth
     That the world masters. Now, in faith, Gratiano,
     You give your wife too unkind a cause of grief:
     An 't were to me, I should be mad at it.

BASS.   [*Aside*] Why, I were best to cut my left hand off,
     And swear I lost the ring defending it.

GRA.   My Lord Bassanio gave his ring away
     Unto the judge that begg'd it, and indeed
     Deserved it too; and then the boy, his clerk,
     That took some pains in writing, he begg'd mine;
     And neither man nor master would take aught
     But the two rings.

POR.   What ring gave you, my lord?
     Not that, I hope, which you received of me.

BASS.   If I could add a lie unto a fault,
     I would deny it; but you see my finger
     Hath not the ring upon it, it is gone.

POR.   Even so void is your false heart of truth.
     By heaven, I will ne'er come in your bed
     Until I see the ring.

NER.   Nor I in yours
     Till I again see mine.

BASS.   Sweet Portia,
     If you did know to whom I gave the ring,
     If you did know for whom I gave the ring,
     And would conceive[10] for what I gave the ring,
     And how unwillingly I left the ring,
     When nought would be accepted but the ring,
     You would abate the strength of your displeasure.

POR.   If you had known the virtue of the ring,
     Or half her worthiness that gave the ring,
     Or your own honour to contain[11] the ring,
     You would not then have parted with the ring.

---

10. *conceive*] form an idea, imagine.
11. *contain*] retain.

What man is there so much unreasonable,
If you had pleased to have defended it
With any terms of zeal, wanted the modesty
To urge the thing held as a ceremony?[12]
Nerissa teaches me what to believe:
I 'll die for 't but some woman had the ring.

BASS. No, by my honour, madam, by my soul,
No woman had it, but a civil doctor,
Which did refuse three thousand ducats of me,
And begg'd the ring; the which I did deny him,
And suffer'd him to go displeased away;
Even he that did uphold the very life
Of my dear friend. What should I say, sweet lady?
I was enforced to send it after him;
I was beset with shame and courtesy;
My honour would not let ingratitude
So much besmear it. Pardon me, good lady;
For, by these blessed candles of the night,
Had you been there, I think you would have begg'd
The ring of me to give the worthy doctor.

POR. Let not that doctor e'er come near my house:
Since he hath got the jewel that I loved,
And that which you did swear to keep for me,
I will become as liberal as you;
I 'll not deny him anything I have,
No, not my body nor my husband's bed:
Know him I shall, I am well sure of it:
Lie not a night from home; watch me like Argus:[13]
If you do not, if I be left alone,
Now, by mine honour, which is yet mine own,
I 'll have that doctor for my bedfellow.

NER. And I his clerk; therefore be well advised
How you do leave me to mine own protection.

GRA. Well, do you so: let not me take him, then;
For if I do, I 'll mar the young clerk's pen.

---

12. *ceremony*] an ornament of sacred import; a solemn trophy.
13. *Argus*] Io's keeper, who had 100 eyes.

ANT. I am the unhappy subject of these quarrels.

POR. Sir, grieve not you; you are welcome notwithstanding.

BASS. Portia, forgive me this enforced wrong;
  And, in the hearing of these many friends,
  I swear to thee, even by thine own fair eyes,
  Wherein I see myself, —

POR.   Mark you but that!
  In both my eyes he doubly sees himself;
  In each eye, one: swear by your double self,
  And there 's an oath of credit.

BASS.   Nay, but hear me:
  Pardon this fault, and by my soul I swear
  I never more will break an oath with thee.

ANT. I once did lend my body for his wealth;
  Which, but for him that had your husband's ring,
  Had quite miscarried: I dare be bound again,
  My soul upon the forfeit, that your lord
  Will never more break faith advisedly.

POR. Then you shall be his surety. Give him this,
  And bid him keep it better than the other.

ANT. Here, Lord Bassanio; swear to keep this ring.

BASS. By heaven, it is the same I gave the doctor!

POR. I had it of him: pardon me, Bassanio;
  For, by this ring, the doctor lay with me.

NER. And pardon me, my gentle Gratiano;
  For that same scrubbed boy, the doctor's clerk,
  In lieu of this last night did lie with me.

GRA. Why, this is like the mending of highways
  In summer, where the ways are fair enough:
  What, are we cuckolds ere we have deserved it?

POR. Speak not so grossly. You are all amazed:
  Here is a letter; read it at your leisure;
  It comes from Padua, from Bellario:
  There you shall find that Portia was the doctor,
  Nerissa there her clerk: Lorenzo here
  Shall witness I set forth as soon as you,
  And even but now return'd; I have not yet
  Enter'd my house. Antonio, you are welcome;

And I have better news in store for you
Than you expect: unseal this letter soon;
There you shall find three of your argosies
Are richly come to harbour suddenly:
You shall not know by what strange accident
I chanced on this letter.

ANT.   I am dumb.

BASS.   Were you the doctor and I knew you not?

GRA.   Were you the clerk that is to make me cuckold?

NER.   Ay, but the clerk that never means to do it,
Unless he live until he be a man.

BASS.   Sweet doctor, you shall be my bedfellow:
When I am absent, then lie with my wife.

ANT.   Sweet lady, you have given me life and living;
For here I read for certain that my ships
Are safely come to road.

POR.   How now, Lorenzo!
My clerk hath some good comforts too for you.

NER.   Ay, and I 'll give them him without a fee.
There do I give to you and Jessica,
From the rich Jew, a special deed of gift,
After his death, of all he dies possess'd of.

LOR.   Fair ladies, you drop manna in the way
Of starved people.

POR.   It is almost morning,
And yet I am sure you are not satisfied
Of these events at full. Let us go in;
And charge us there upon inter'gatories,
And we will answer all things faithfully.

GRA.   Let it be so: the first inter'gatory
That my Nerissa shall be sworn on is,
Whether till the next night she had rather stay,
Or go to bed now, being two hours to day:
But were the day come, I should wish it dark,
That I were couching with the doctor's clerk.
Well, while I live I 'll fear no other thing
So sore as keeping safe Nerissa's ring.   [*Exeunt.*]